W9-DAM-924

Reading Level: 2.9

Point Value: .5

JUL 30 2013

Marshall County Public Library
@ Hardin
Hardin, KY 42048

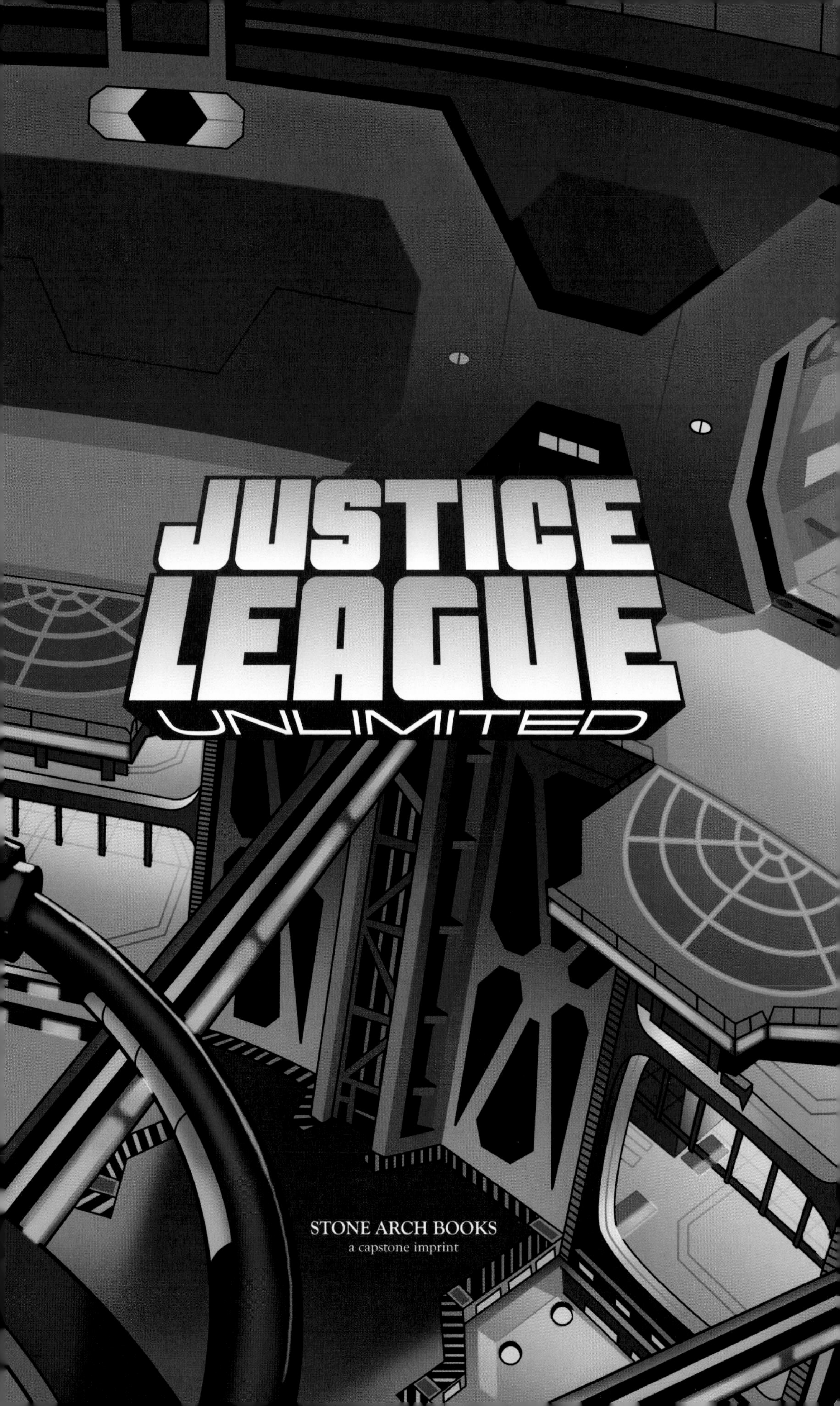

JUSTICE LEAGUE UNLIMITED

STONE ARCH BOOKS
a capstone imprint

STONE ARCH BOOKS™

Published in 2013
A Capstone Imprint
1710 Roe Crest Drive
North Mankato, MN 56003
www.capstonepub.com

Originally published by DC Comics in the U.S. in single
magazine form as Justice League Unlimited #2.
Copyright © 2013 DC Comics. All Rights Reserved.

DC Comics
1700 Broadway, New York, NY 10019
A Warner Bros. Entertainment Company

No part of this publication may be reproduced in
whole or in part, or stored in a retrieval system, or
transmitted in any form or by any means, electronic,
mechanical, photocopying, recording, or otherwise,
without written permission.

Printed in China by Nordica.
1012/CA21201277
092012   006935NORDS13

Cataloging-in-Publication Data is available at the Library of
Congress website:
ISBN: 978-1-4342-4714-8 (library binding)

Summary: Guest-starring Booster Gold and Steel! The
League battles the Royal Flush Gang in Las Vegas, and
Booster learns why the team pays Superman so much
respect.

STONE ARCH BOOKS

Ashley C. Andersen Zantop *Publisher*
Michael Dahl *Editorial Director*
Donald Lemke *Editor*
Heather Kindseth *Creative Director*
Bob Lentz *Designer*
Kathy McColley *Production Specialist*

DC COMICS

Tom Palmer Jr. *Original U.S. Editor*

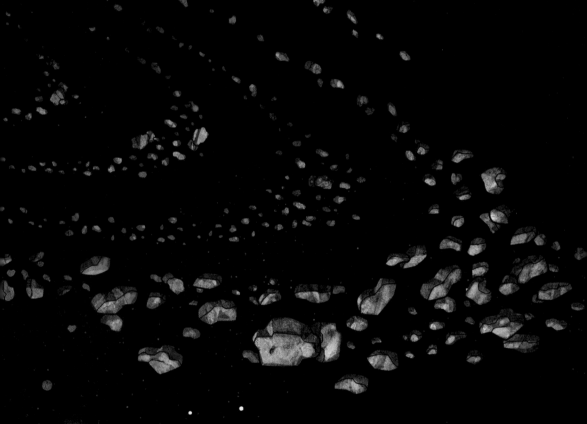

JUSTICE LEAGUE UNLIMITED

POKER FACE

Adam Beechen...................................... writer
Ethen Beavers.. artist
Heroic Age .... colorist
Nick J. Napolitano ....letterer

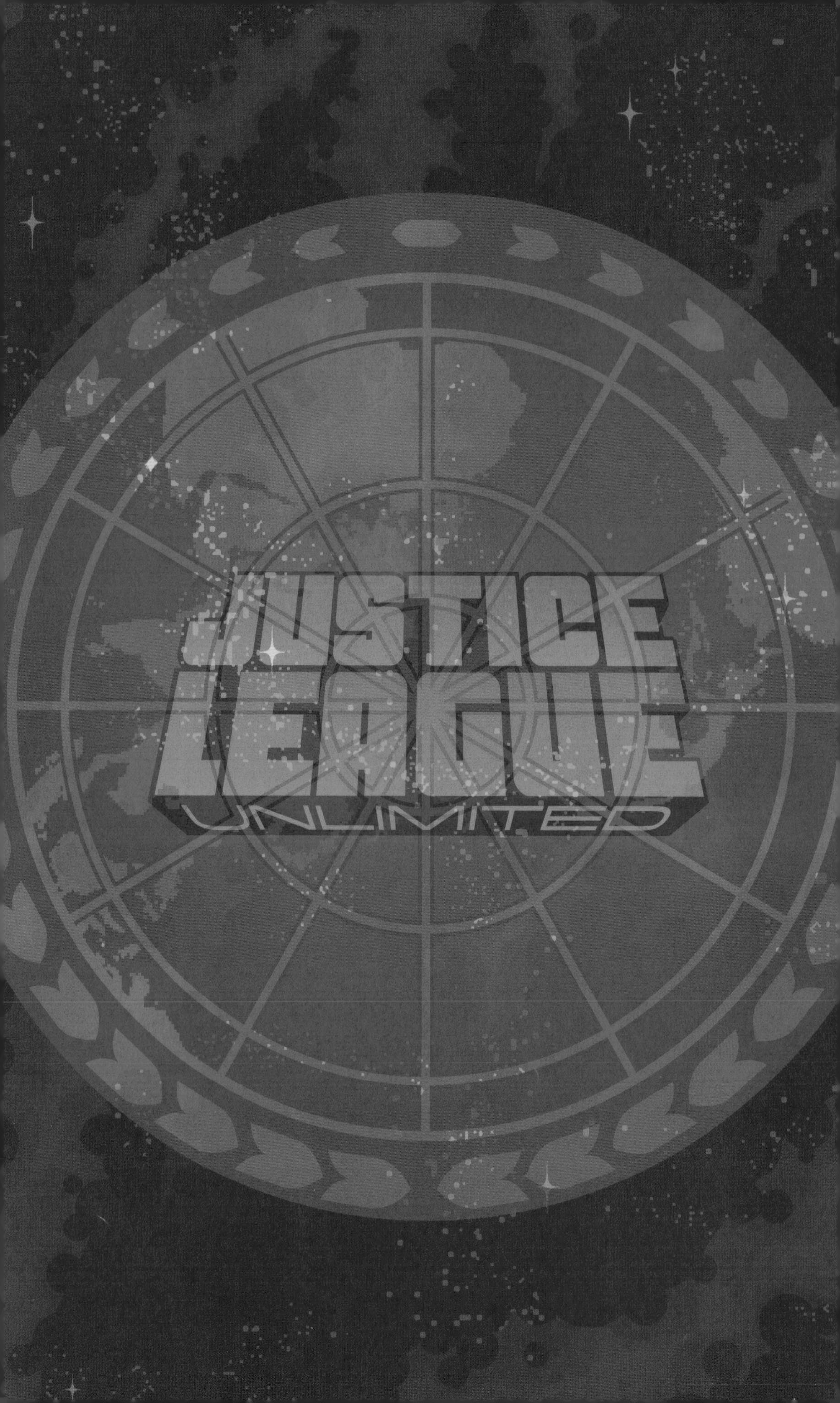
JUSTICE
LEAGUE
UNLIMITED

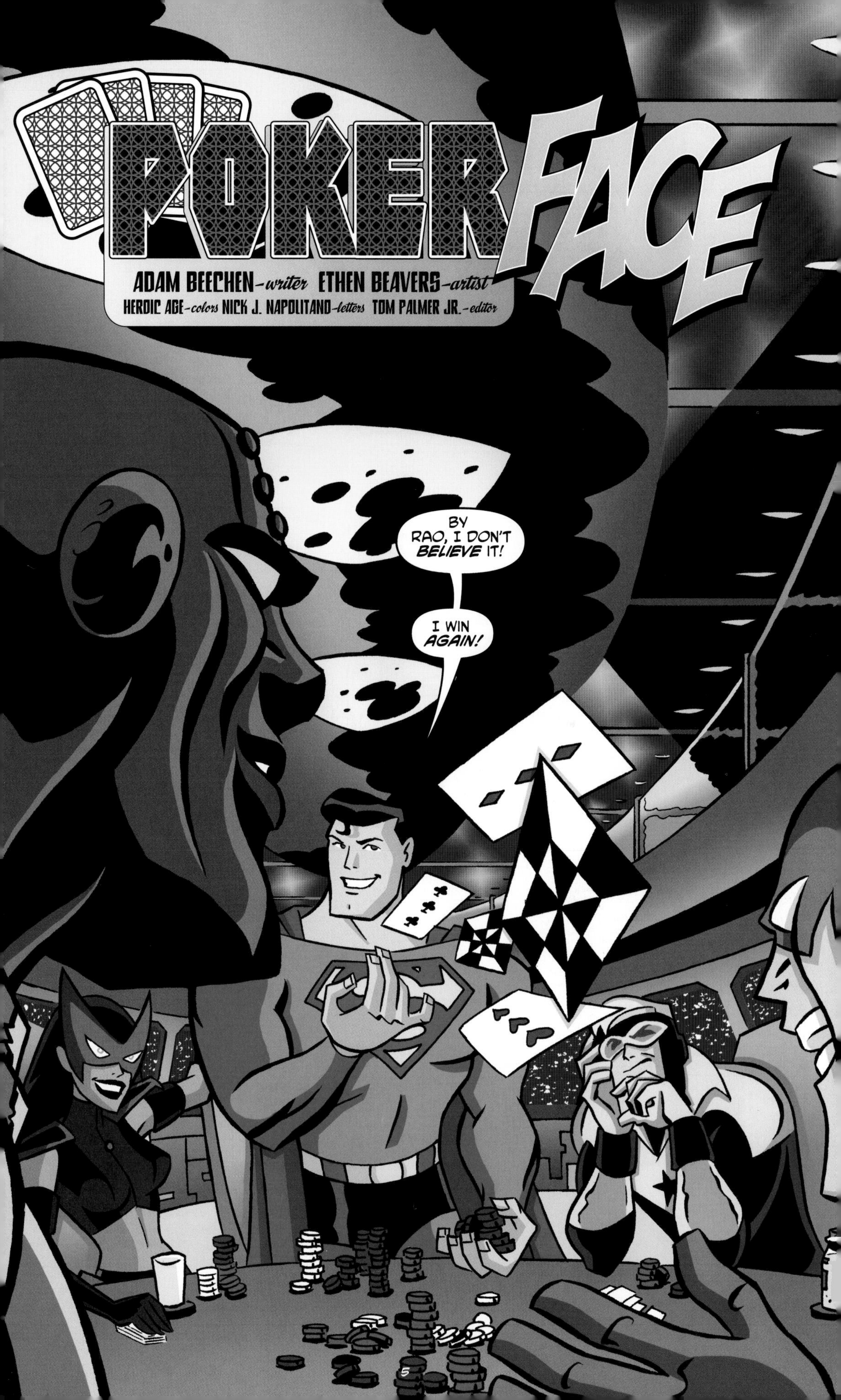

POKER FACE
ADAM BEECHEN–writer ETHEN BEAVERS–artist
HEROIC AGE–colors NICK J. NAPOLITANO–letters TOM PALMER JR.–editor
BY RAO, I DON'T BELIEVE IT!
I WIN AGAIN!

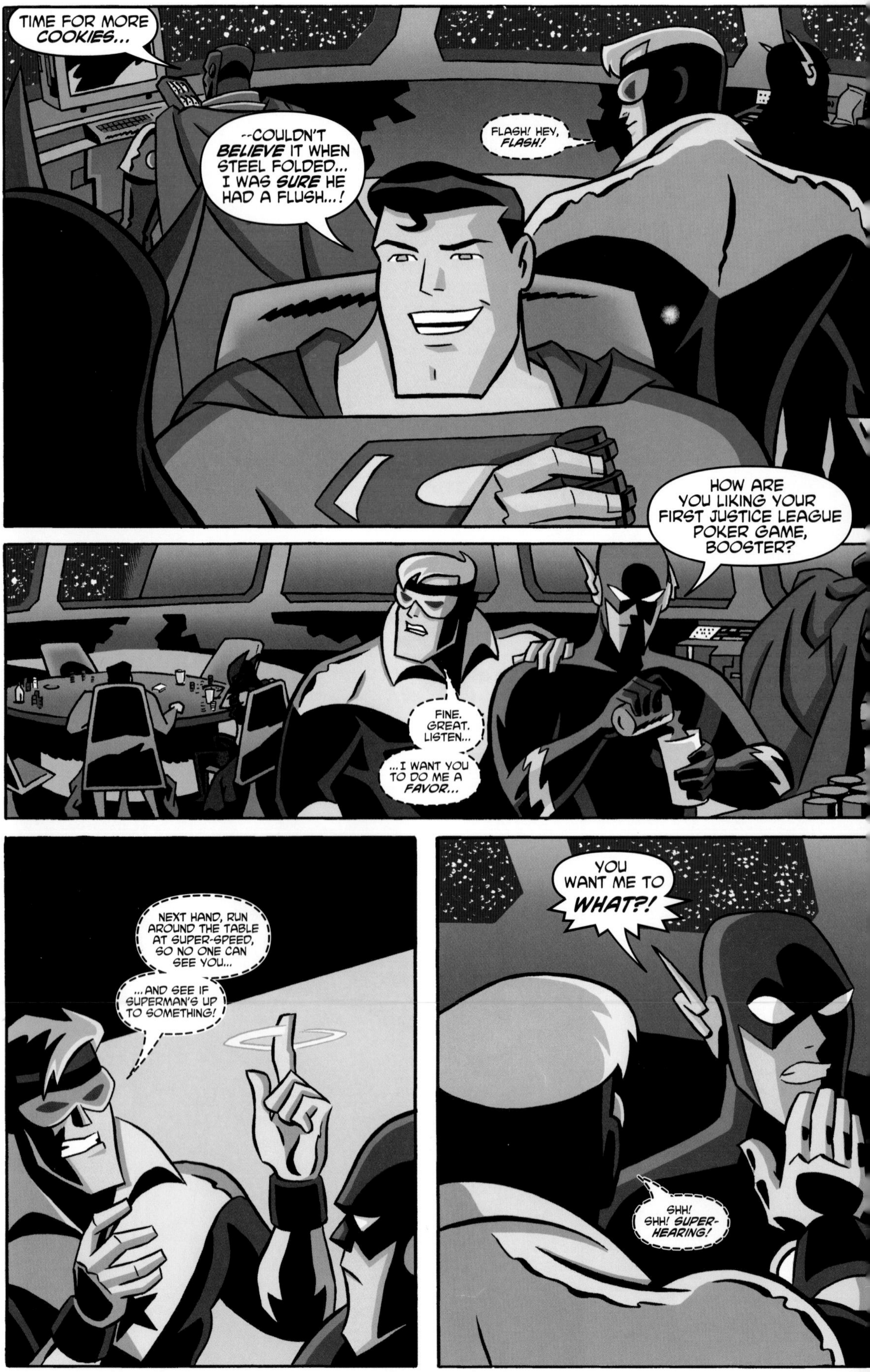
TIME FOR MORE COOKIES...
--COULDN'T BELIEVE IT WHEN STEEL FOLDED... I WAS SURE HE HAD A FLUSH...!
FLASH! HEY, FLASH!
HOW ARE YOU LIKING YOUR FIRST JUSTICE LEAGUE POKER GAME, BOOSTER?
FINE. GREAT. LISTEN...
...I WANT YOU TO DO ME A FAVOR...
NEXT HAND, RUN AROUND THE TABLE AT SUPER-SPEED, SO NO ONE CAN SEE YOU...
...AND SEE IF SUPERMAN'S UP TO SOMETHING!
YOU WANT ME TO WHAT?!
SHH! SHH! SUPER-HEARING!

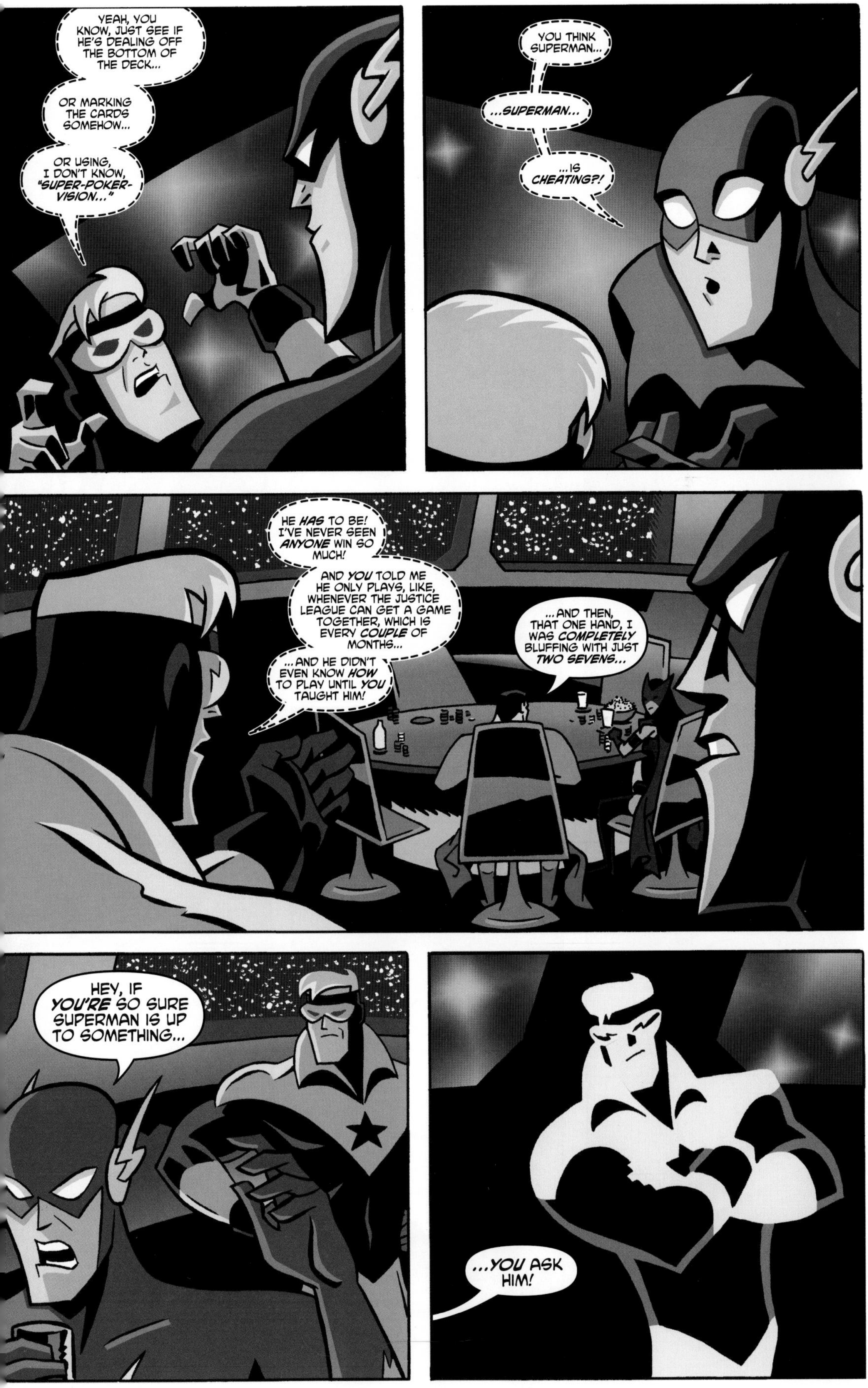
YEAH, YOU KNOW, JUST SEE IF HE'S DEALING OFF THE BOTTOM OF THE DECK...
OR MARKING THE CARDS SOMEHOW...
OR USING, I DON'T KNOW, "SUPER-POKER-VISION..."
YOU THINK SUPERMAN...
...SUPERMAN...
...IS CHEATING?!
HE HAS TO BE! I'VE NEVER SEEN ANYONE WIN SO MUCH!
AND YOU TOLD ME HE ONLY PLAYS, LIKE, WHENEVER THE JUSTICE LEAGUE CAN GET A GAME TOGETHER, WHICH IS EVERY COUPLE OF MONTHS...
...AND HE DIDN'T EVEN KNOW HOW TO PLAY UNTIL YOU TAUGHT HIM!
...AND THEN, THAT ONE HAND, I WAS COMPLETELY BLUFFING WITH JUST TWO SEVENS...
HEY, IF YOU'RE SO SURE SUPERMAN IS UP TO SOMETHING...
...YOU ASK HIM!

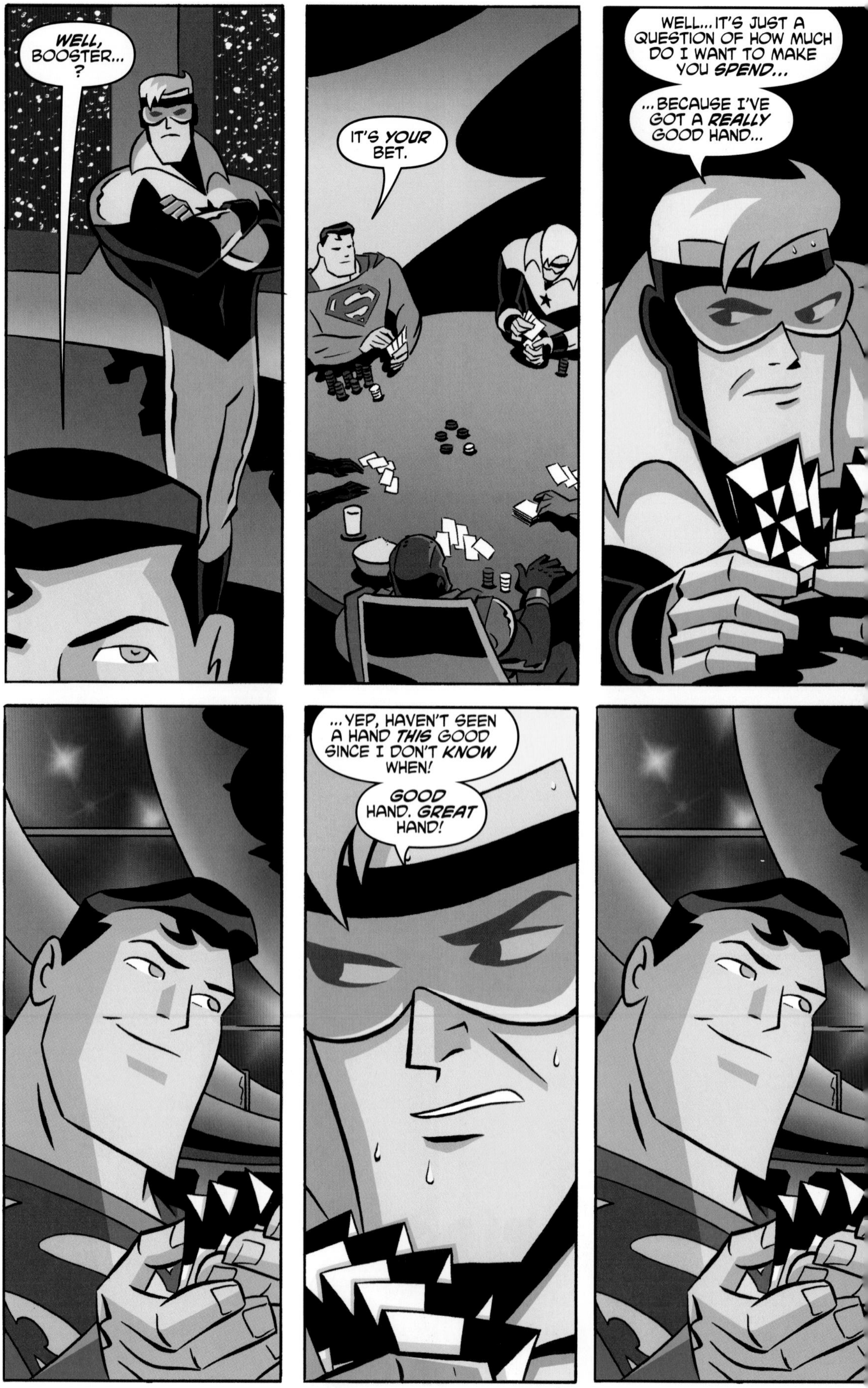

WELL, BOOSTER... ?
IT'S YOUR BET.
WELL... IT'S JUST A QUESTION OF HOW MUCH DO I WANT TO MAKE YOU SPEND...
...BECAUSE I'VE GOT A REALLY GOOD HAND...
...YEP, HAVEN'T SEEN A HAND THIS GOOD SINCE I DON'T KNOW WHEN!
GOOD HAND. GREAT HAND!

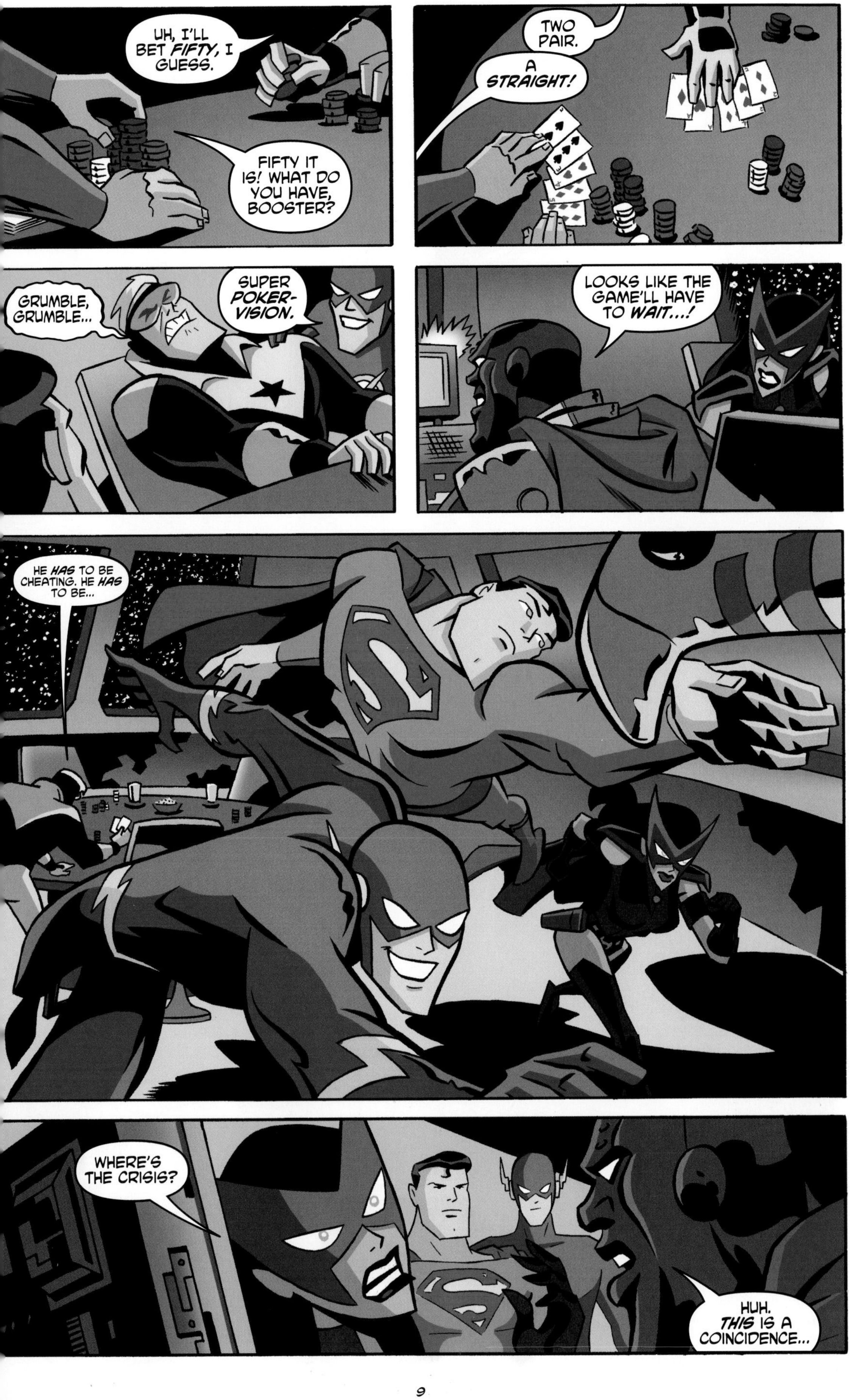
UH, I'LL BET *FIFTY*, I GUESS.
FIFTY IT IS! WHAT DO YOU HAVE, BOOSTER?
TWO PAIR.
A *STRAIGHT!*
GRUMBLE, GRUMBLE...
SUPER *POKER-VISION.*
LOOKS LIKE THE GAME'LL HAVE TO *WAIT...!*
HE *HAS* TO BE CHEATING. HE *HAS* TO BE...
WHERE'S THE CRISIS?
HUH. *THIS* IS A COINCIDENCE...

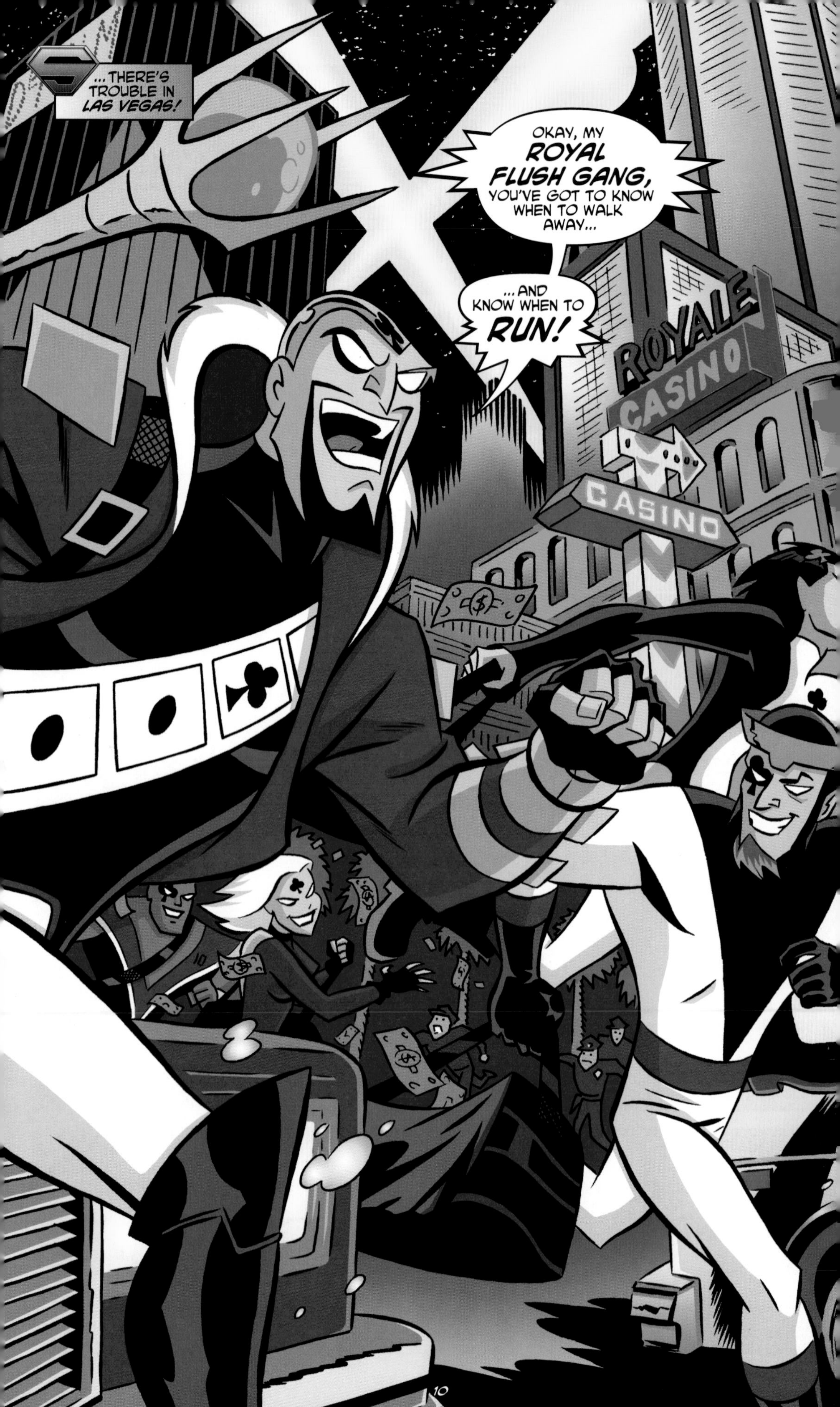
...THERE'S TROUBLE IN LAS VEGAS!
OKAY, MY ROYAL FLUSH GANG, YOU'VE GOT TO KNOW WHEN TO WALK AWAY...
...AND KNOW WHEN TO RUN!
ROYALE CASINO
CASINO

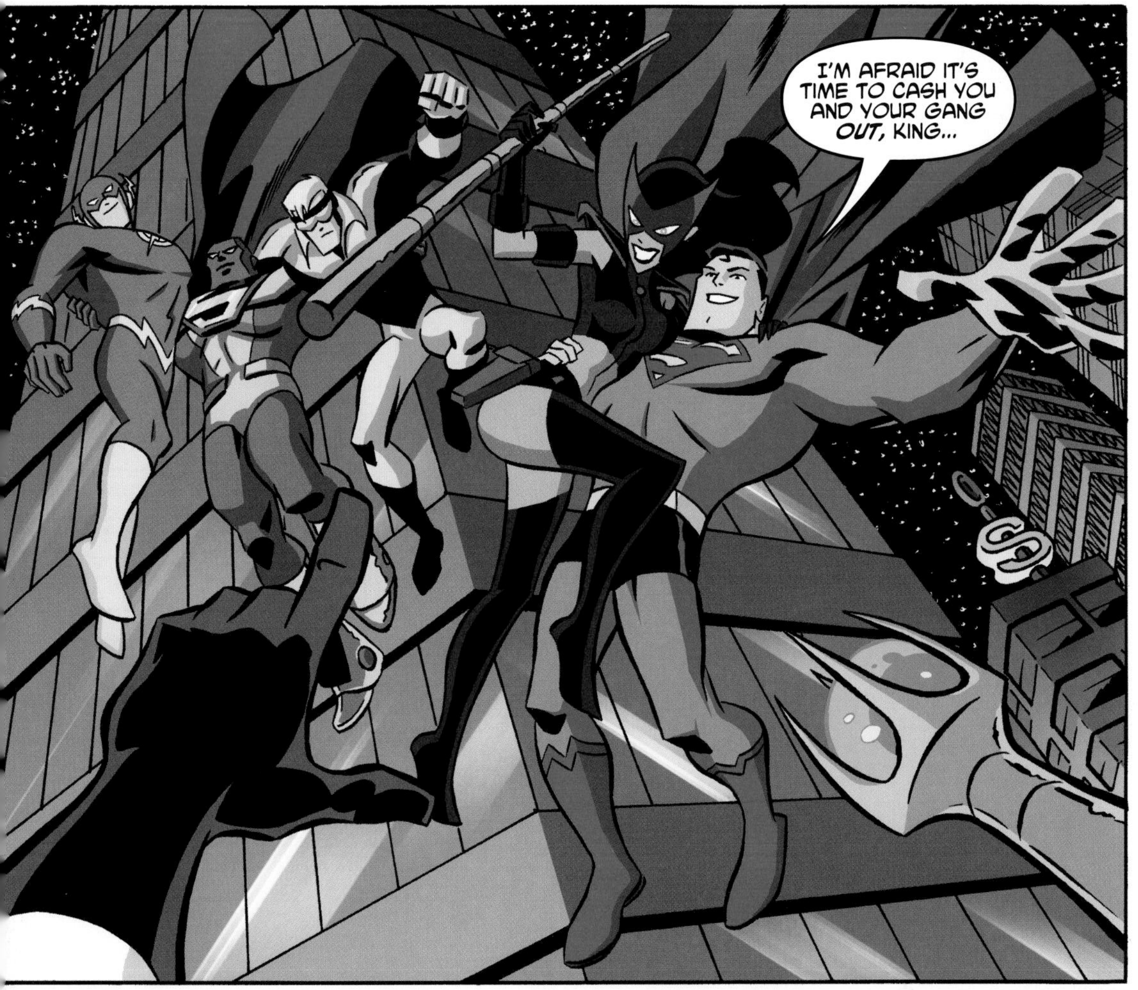
I'M AFRAID IT'S TIME TO CASH YOU AND YOUR GANG *OUT*, KING...

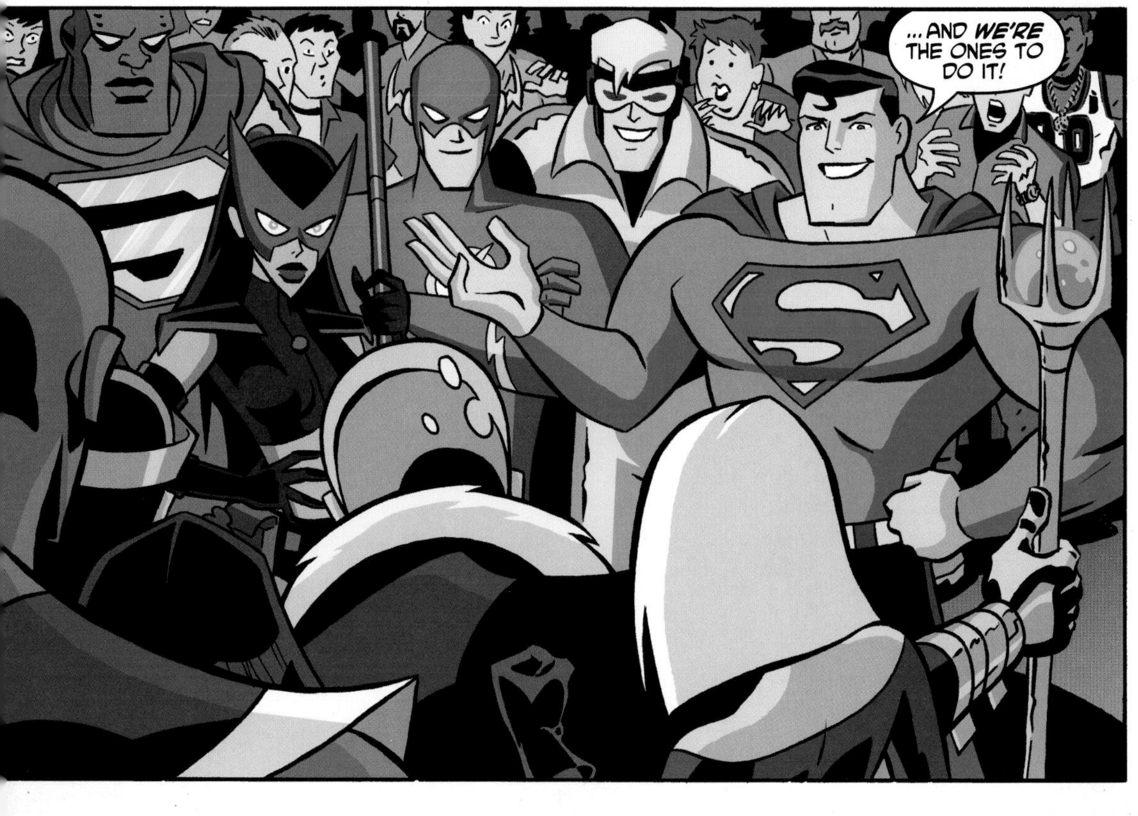
...AND *WE'RE* THE ONES TO DO IT!

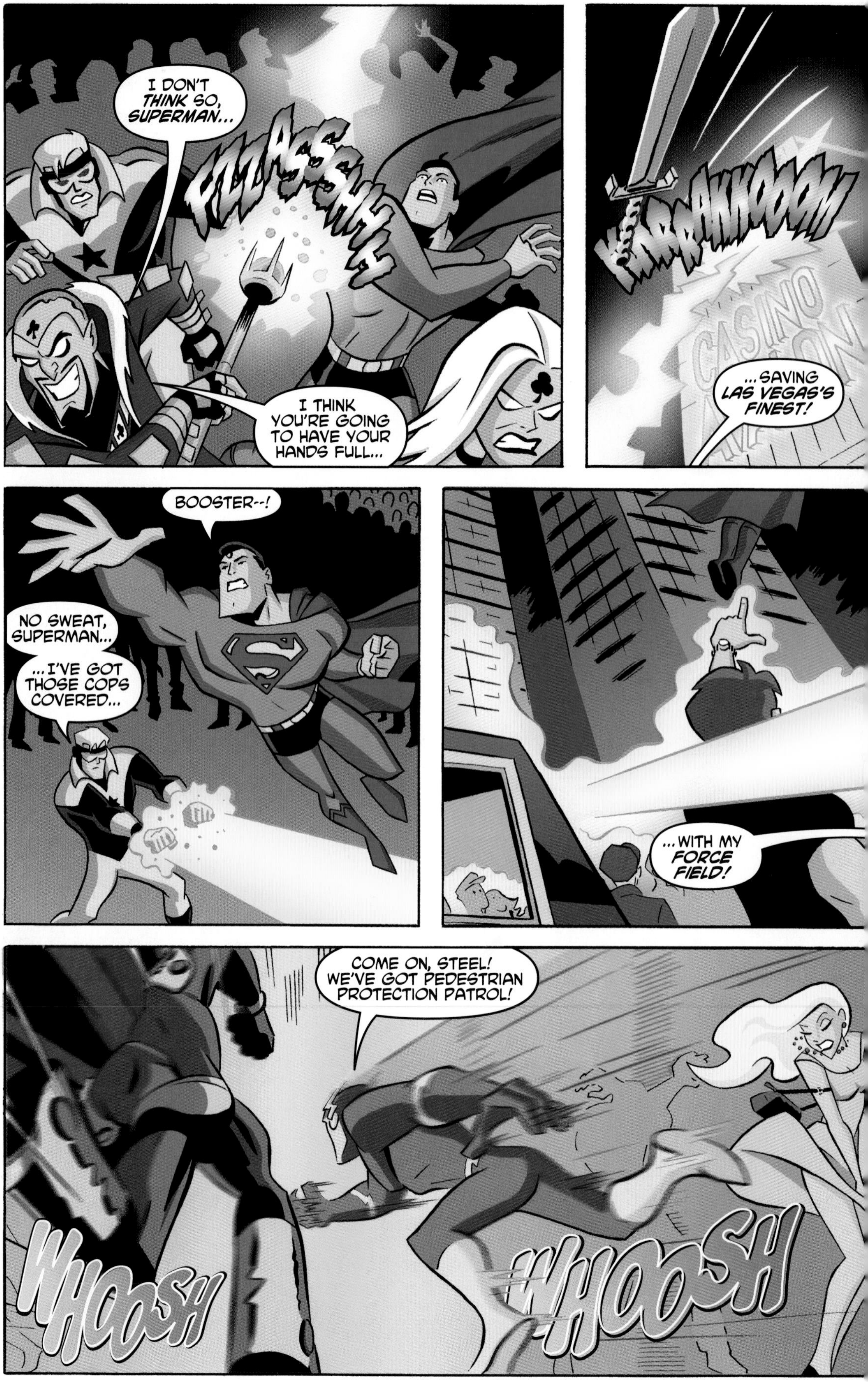
I DON'T THINK SO, SUPERMAN...
FZZASSSHH
I THINK YOU'RE GOING TO HAVE YOUR HANDS FULL...
KRRAKKOOOM
CASINO
...SAVING LAS VEGAS'S FINEST!
BOOSTER--!
NO SWEAT, SUPERMAN...
...I'VE GOT THOSE COPS COVERED...
...WITH MY FORCE FIELD!
COME ON, STEEL! WE'VE GOT PEDESTRIAN PROTECTION PATROL!
WHOOSH
WHOOSH

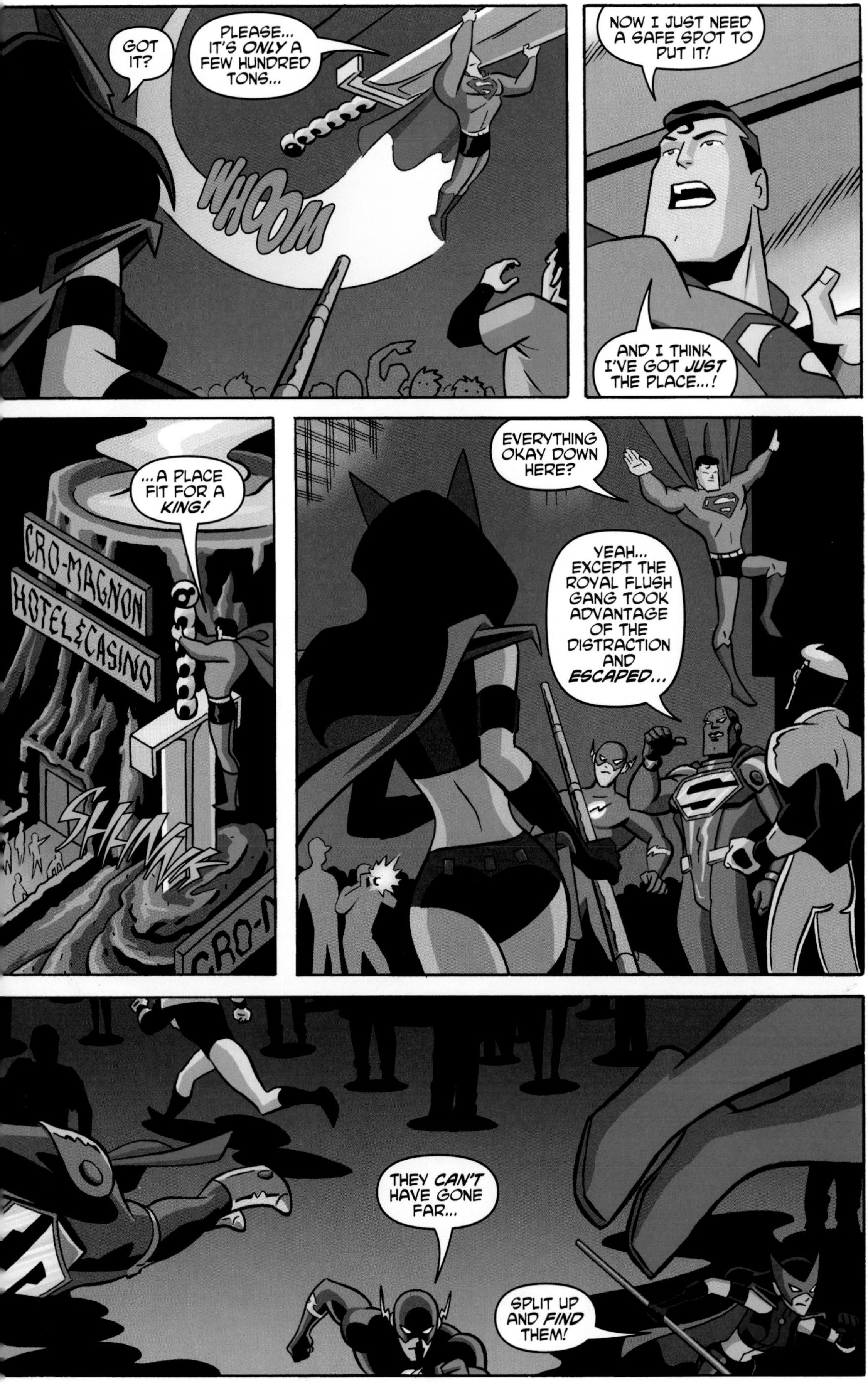
GOT IT?
PLEASE... IT'S *ONLY* A FEW HUNDRED TONS...
WHOOM
NOW I JUST NEED A SAFE SPOT TO PUT IT!
AND I THINK I'VE GOT *JUST* THE PLACE...!
...A PLACE FIT FOR A *KING!*
CRO-MAGNON
HOTEL & CASINO
SHUNK
CRO-M
EVERYTHING OKAY DOWN HERE?
YEAH... EXCEPT THE ROYAL FLUSH GANG TOOK ADVANTAGE OF THE DISTRACTION AND *ESCAPED...*
THEY *CAN'T* HAVE GONE FAR...
SPLIT UP AND *FIND* THEM!

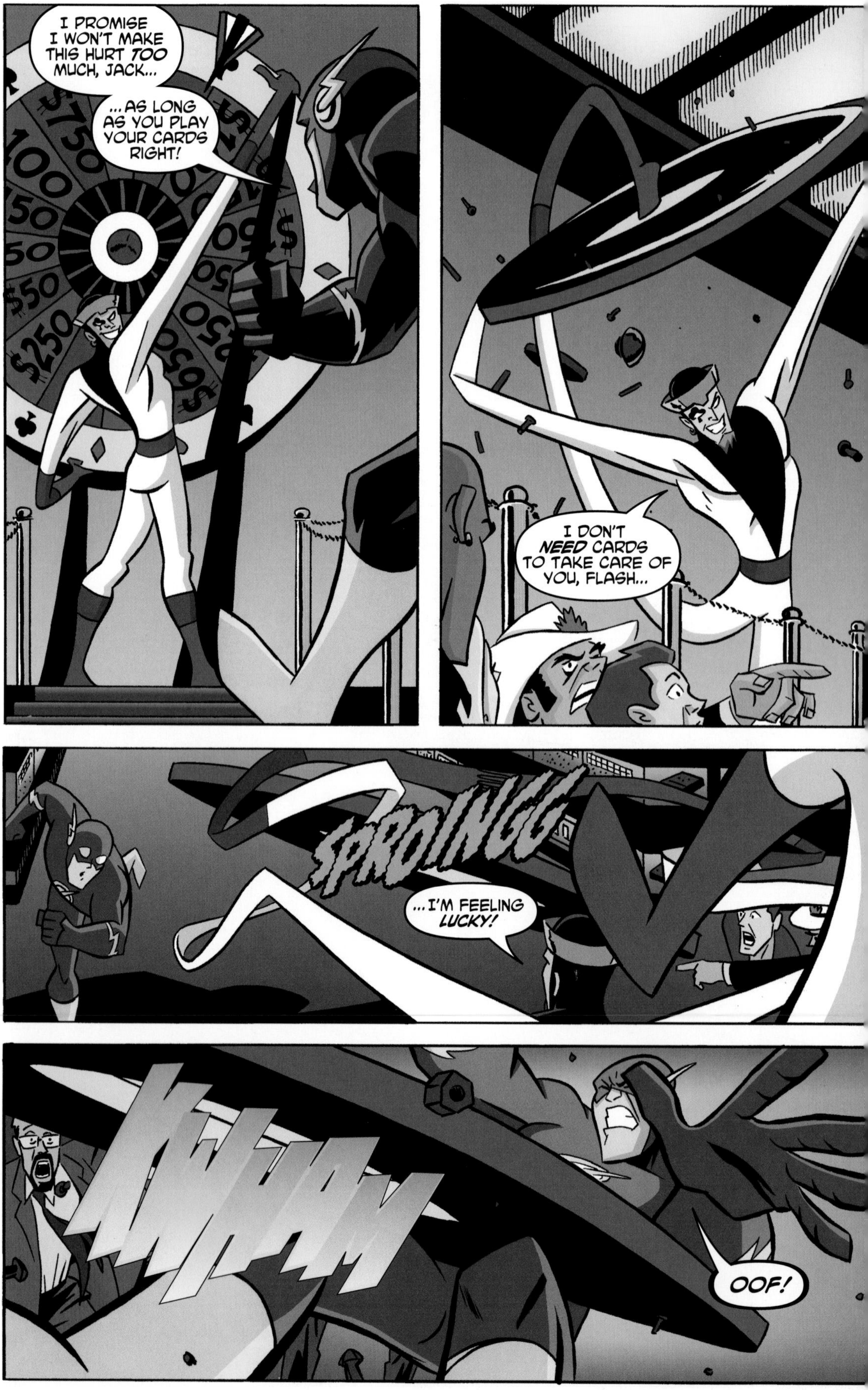
I PROMISE I WON'T MAKE THIS HURT TOO MUCH, JACK...
...AS LONG AS YOU PLAY YOUR CARDS RIGHT!
I DON'T NEED CARDS TO TAKE CARE OF YOU, FLASH...
SPROINGG
...I'M FEELING LUCKY!
WHAM
OOF!

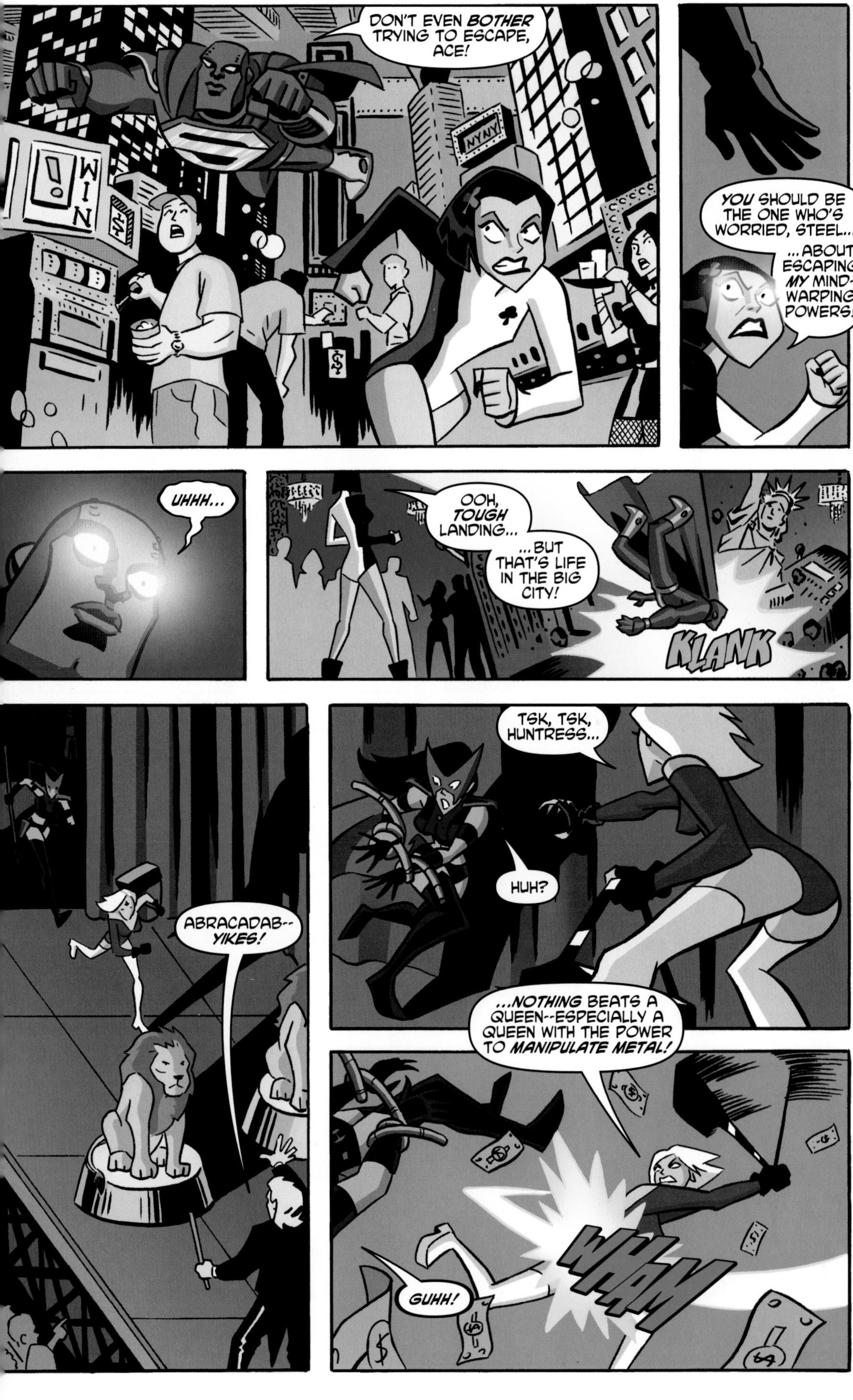

DON'T EVEN *BOTHER* TRYING TO ESCAPE, ACE!
WIN
NYNY
YOU SHOULD BE THE ONE WHO'S WORRIED, STEEL...
...ABOUT ESCAPING *MY* MIND-WARPING POWERS!
UHHH...
OOH, *TOUGH* LANDING...
...BUT THAT'S LIFE IN THE BIG CITY!
KLANK
ABRACADAB-- *YIKES!*
TSK, TSK, HUNTRESS...
HUH?
...*NOTHING* BEATS A QUEEN--ESPECIALLY A QUEEN WITH THE POWER TO *MANIPULATE METAL!*
WHAM
GUHH!

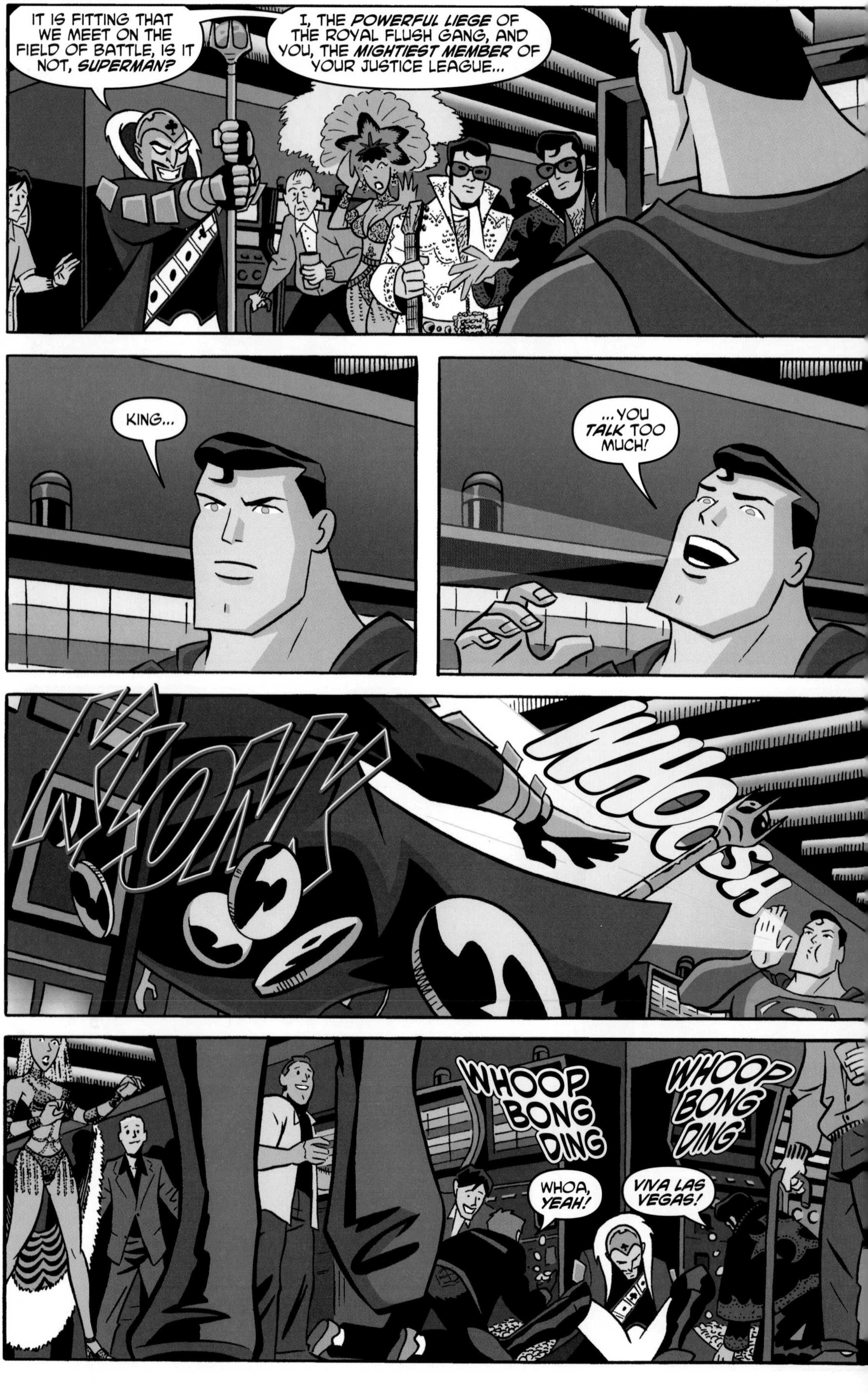

IT IS FITTING THAT WE MEET ON THE FIELD OF BATTLE, IS IT NOT, *SUPERMAN?*
I, THE *POWERFUL LIEGE* OF THE ROYAL FLUSH GANG, AND YOU, THE *MIGHTIEST MEMBER* OF YOUR JUSTICE LEAGUE...
KING...
...YOU *TALK* TOO MUCH!
KLONK
WHOOSH
WHOOP BONG DING
WHOOP BONG DING
WHOA, YEAH!
VIVA LAS VEGAS!

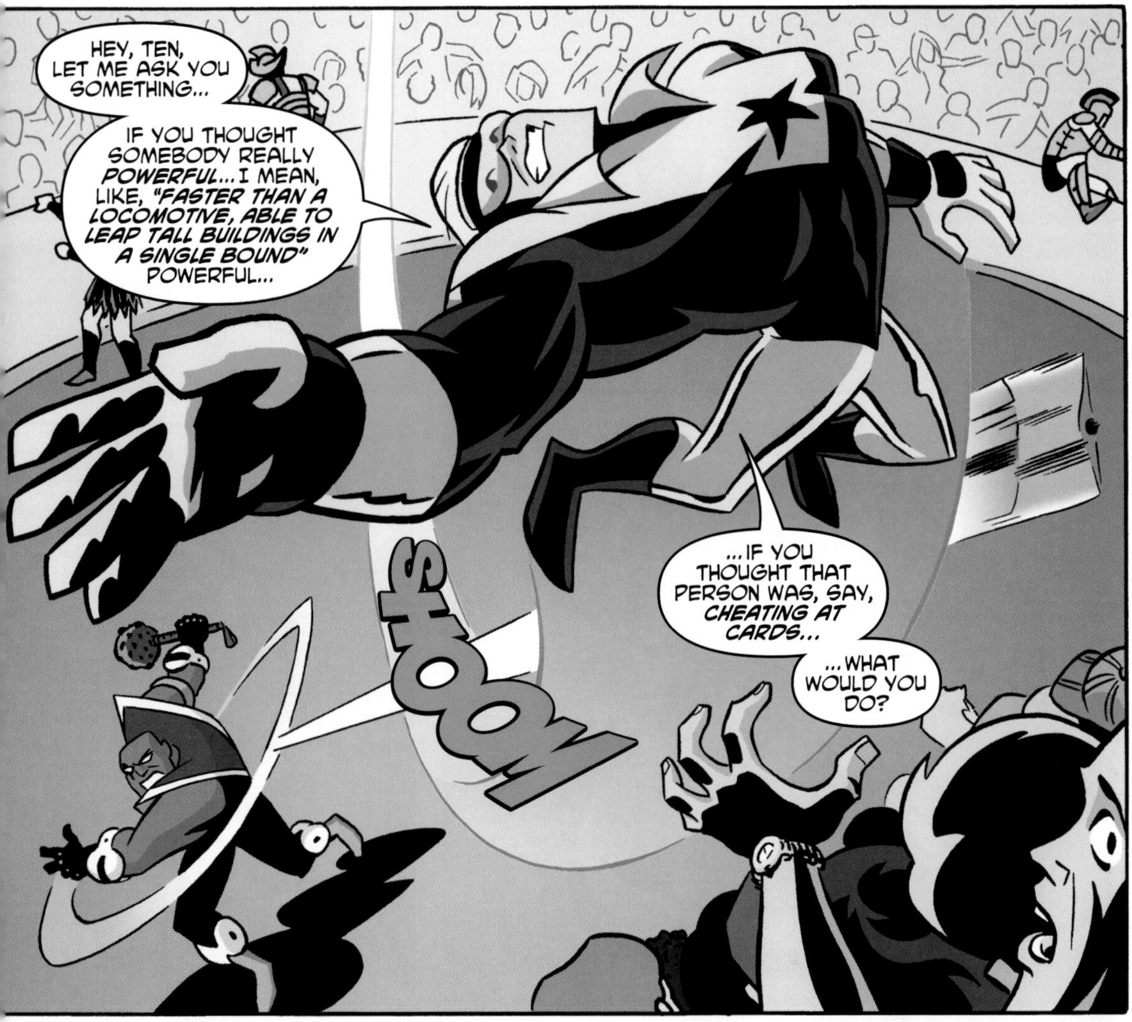
HEY, TEN, LET ME ASK YOU SOMETHING...
IF YOU THOUGHT SOMEBODY REALLY *POWERFUL*... I MEAN, LIKE, *"FASTER THAN A LOCOMOTIVE, ABLE TO LEAP TALL BUILDINGS IN A SINGLE BOUND"* POWERFUL...
SHOOM
...IF YOU THOUGHT THAT PERSON WAS, SAY, *CHEATING AT CARDS...*
...WHAT WOULD YOU DO?

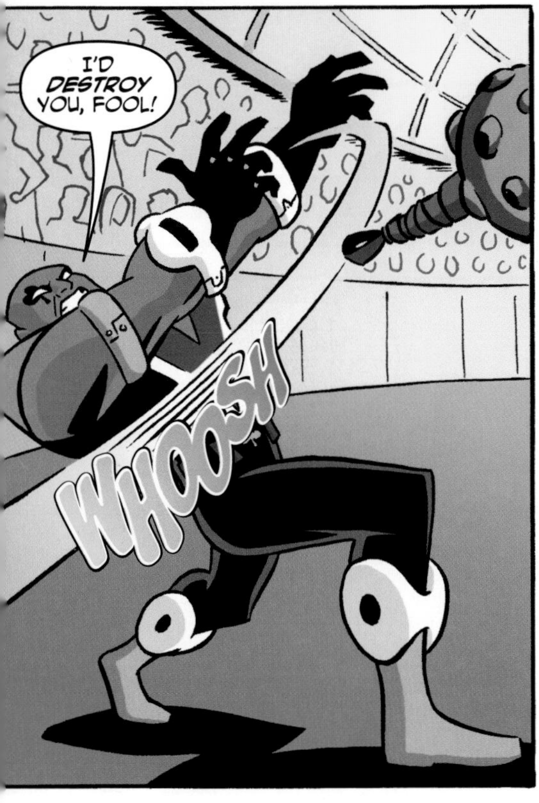
I'D *DESTROY* YOU, FOOL!
WHOOSH

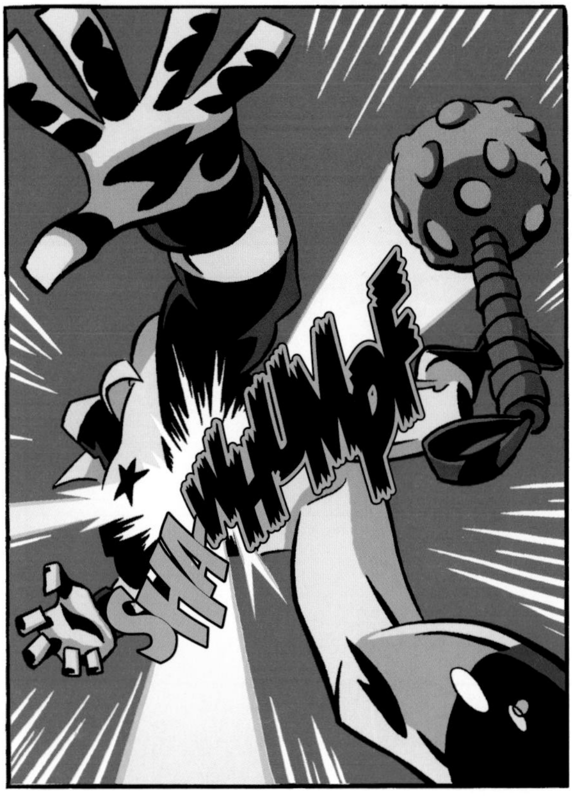
SHA WHUMP

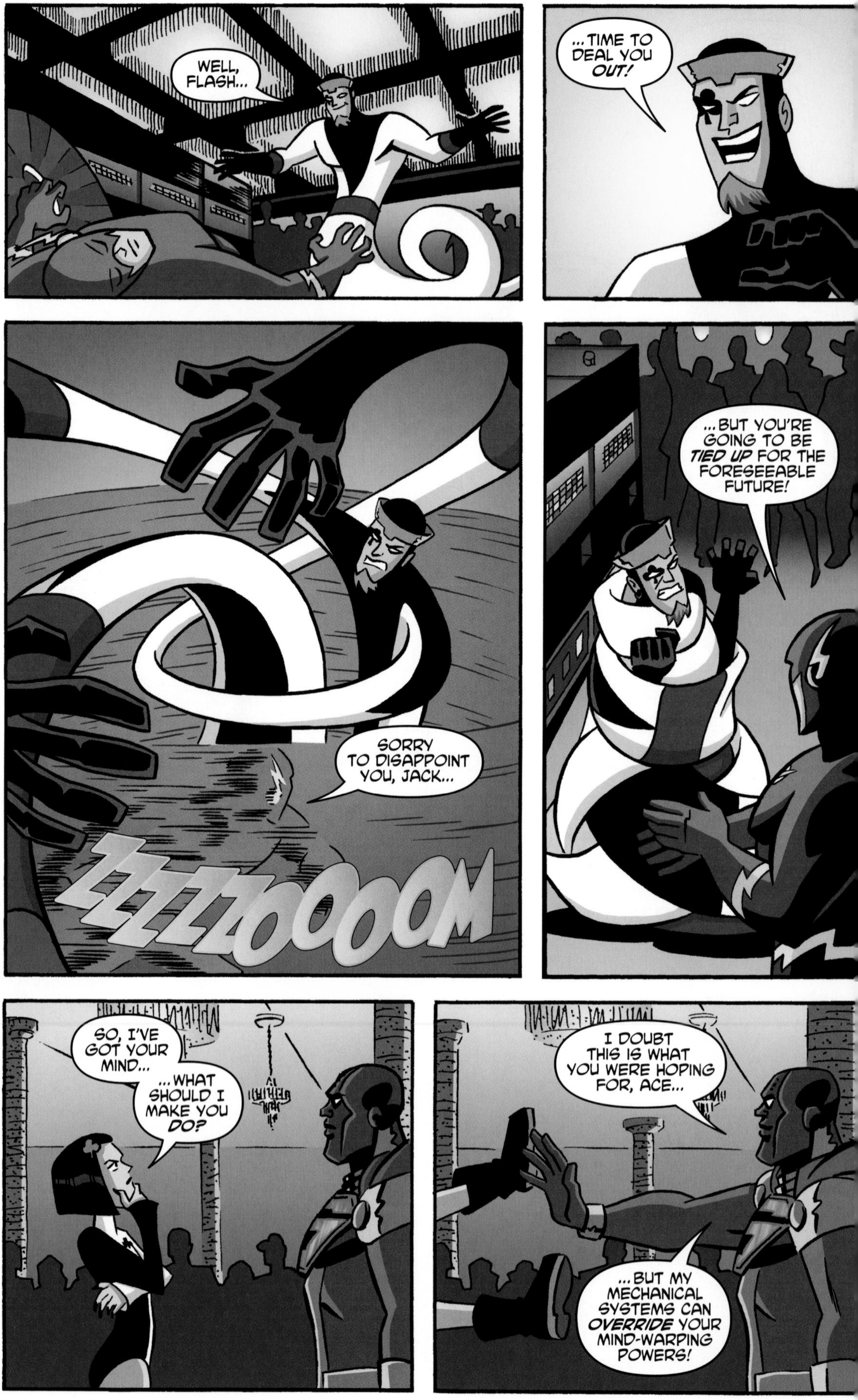
WELL, FLASH...
...TIME TO DEAL YOU OUT!
SORRY TO DISAPPOINT YOU, JACK...
ZZZZZOOOOM
...BUT YOU'RE GOING TO BE TIED UP FOR THE FORESEEABLE FUTURE!
SO, I'VE GOT YOUR MIND...
...WHAT SHOULD I MAKE YOU DO?
I DOUBT THIS IS WHAT YOU WERE HOPING FOR, ACE...
...BUT MY MECHANICAL SYSTEMS CAN OVERRIDE YOUR MIND-WARPING POWERS!

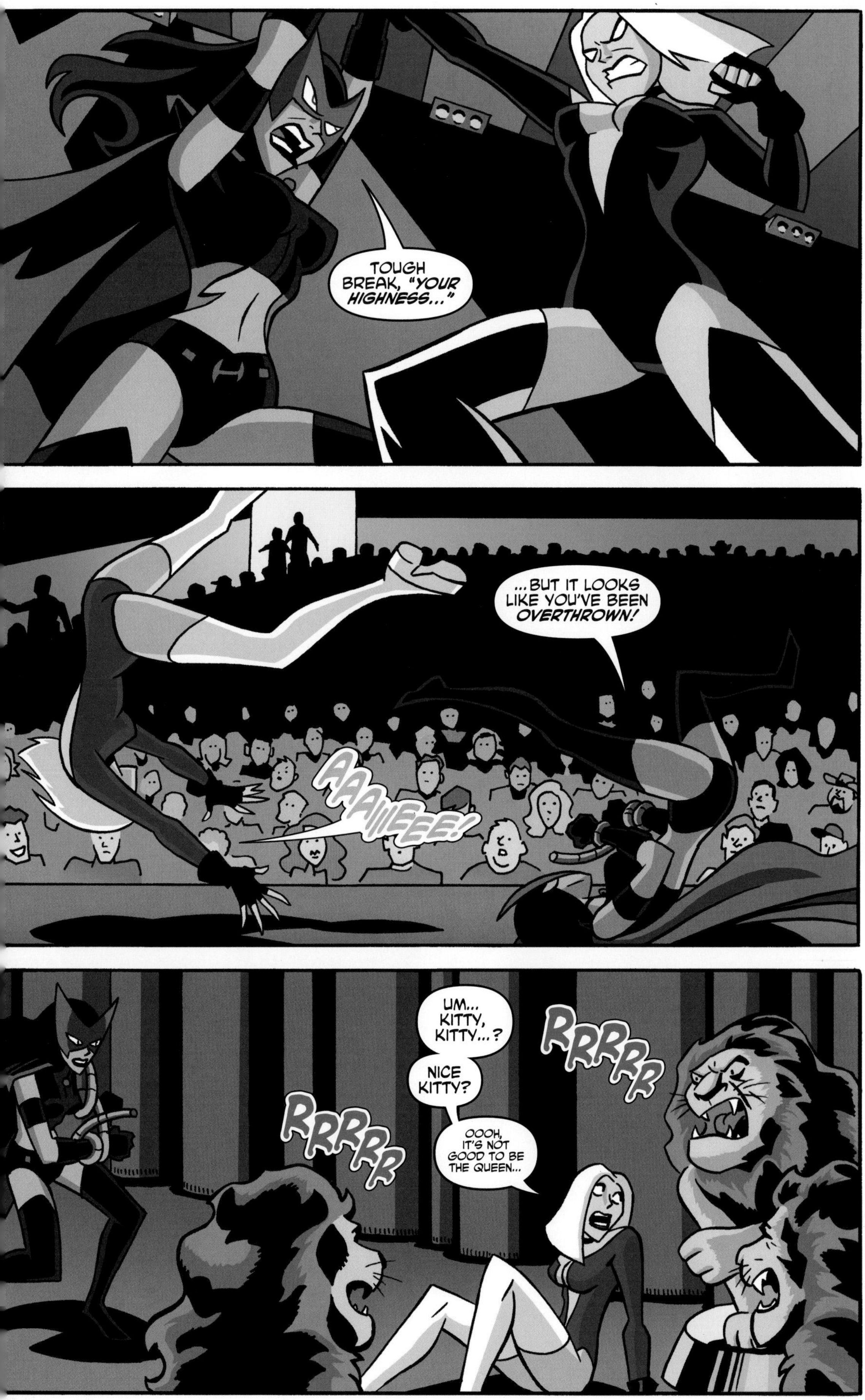

TOUGH BREAK, "YOUR HIGHNESS..."
...BUT IT LOOKS LIKE YOU'VE BEEN OVERTHROWN!
AAAIIIEEEE!
UM... KITTY, KITTY...?
RRRRR
NICE KITTY?
RRRRR
OOOH, IT'S NOT GOOD TO BE THE QUEEN...

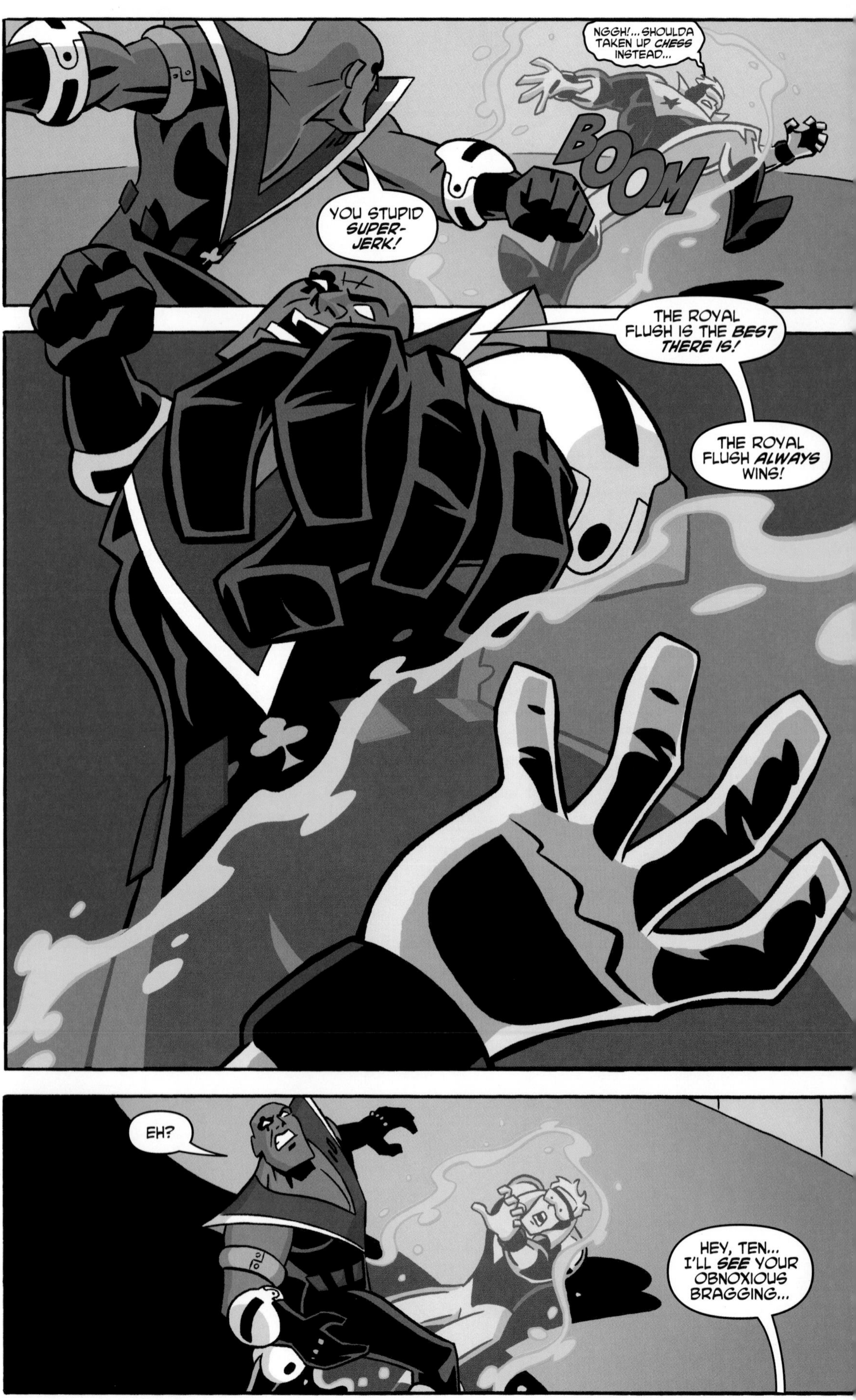
NGGH!... SHOULDA TAKEN UP CHESS INSTEAD...
BOOM
YOU STUPID SUPER-JERK!
THE ROYAL FLUSH IS THE BEST THERE IS!
THE ROYAL FLUSH ALWAYS WINS!
EH?
HEY, TEN... I'LL SEE YOUR OBNOXIOUS BRAGGING...

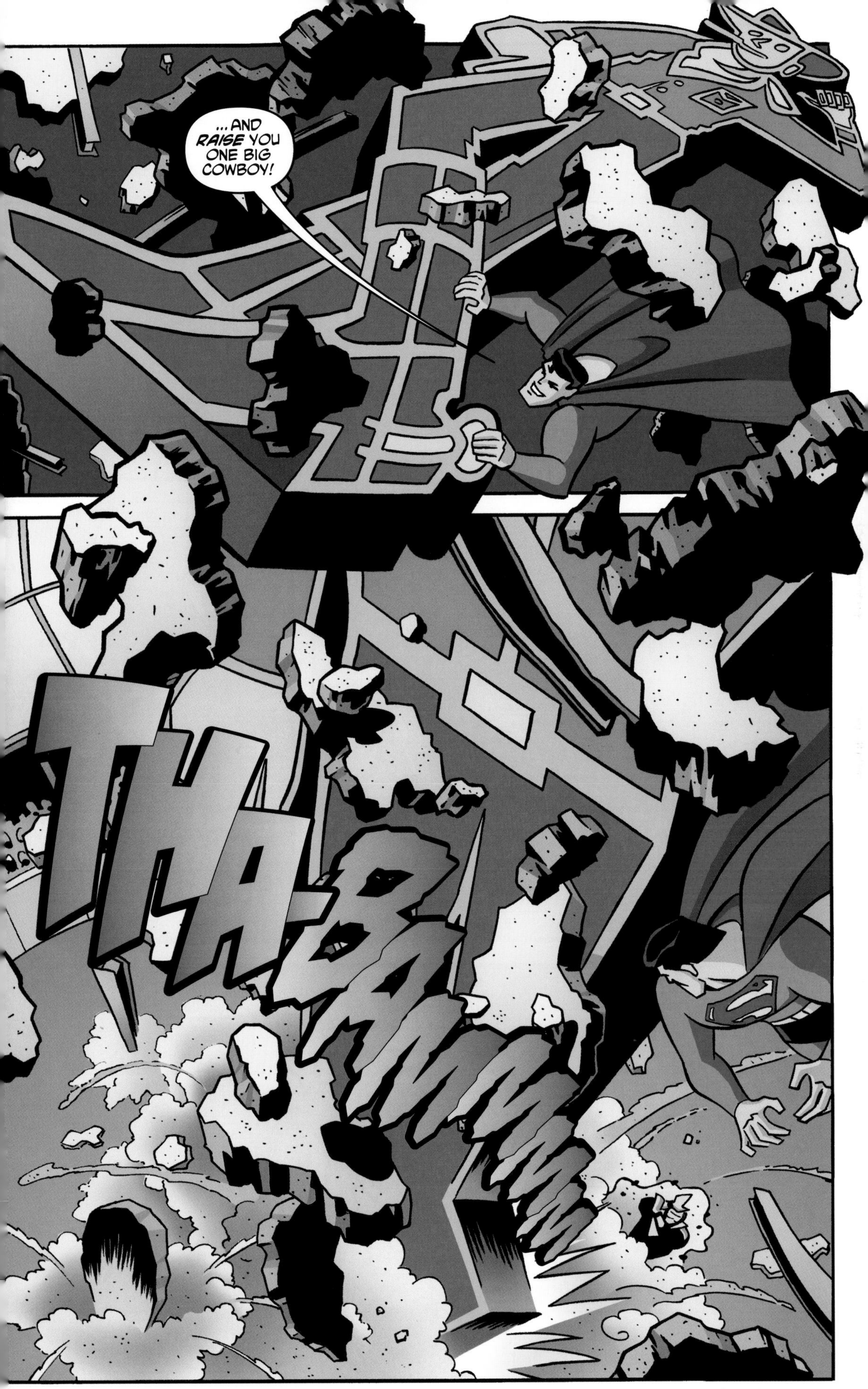
...AND RAISE YOU ONE BIG COWBOY!
THA-BAMM

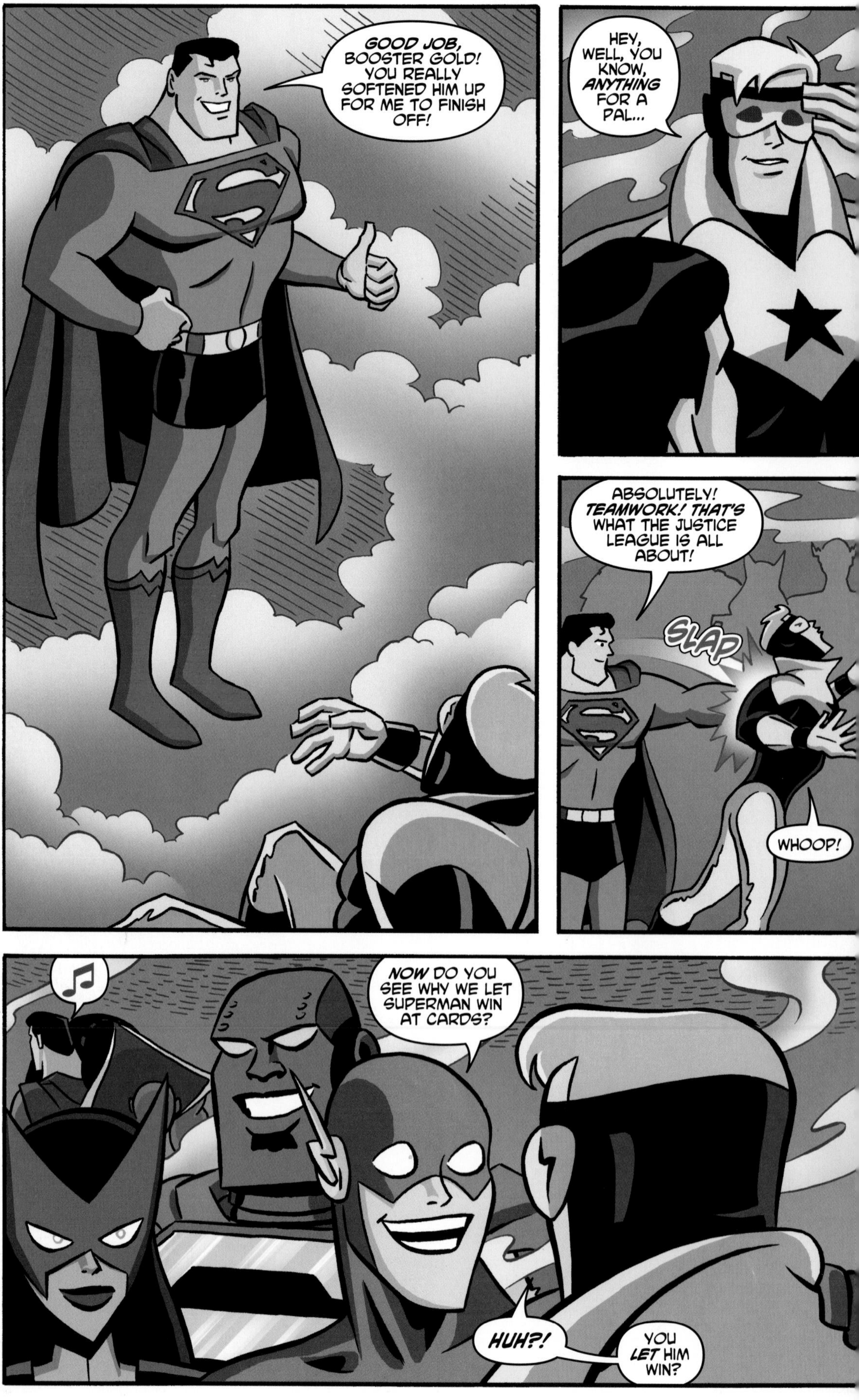
GOOD JOB, BOOSTER GOLD! YOU REALLY SOFTENED HIM UP FOR ME TO FINISH OFF!
HEY, WELL, YOU KNOW, ANYTHING FOR A PAL...
ABSOLUTELY! TEAMWORK! THAT'S WHAT THE JUSTICE LEAGUE IS ALL ABOUT!
SLAP
WHOOP!
♫
NOW DO YOU SEE WHY WE LET SUPERMAN WIN AT CARDS?
HUH?!
YOU LET HIM WIN?

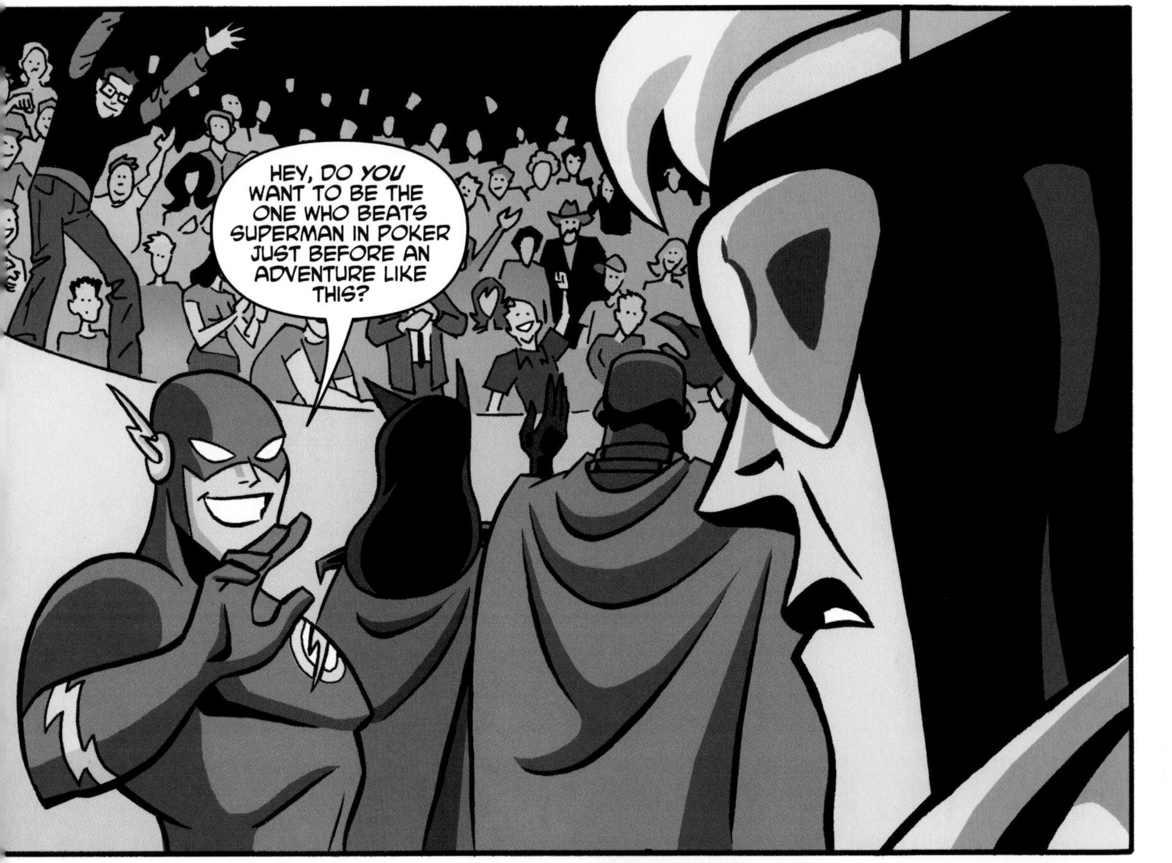
HEY, DO *YOU* WANT TO BE THE ONE WHO BEATS SUPERMAN IN POKER JUST BEFORE AN ADVENTURE LIKE THIS?

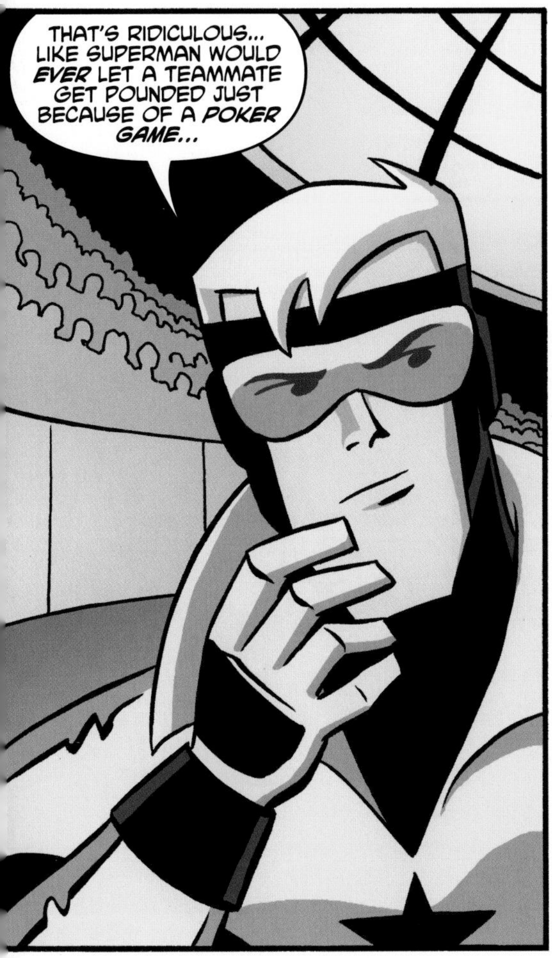
THAT'S RIDICULOUS... LIKE SUPERMAN WOULD ***EVER*** LET A TEAMMATE GET POUNDED JUST BECAUSE OF A ***POKER GAME...***

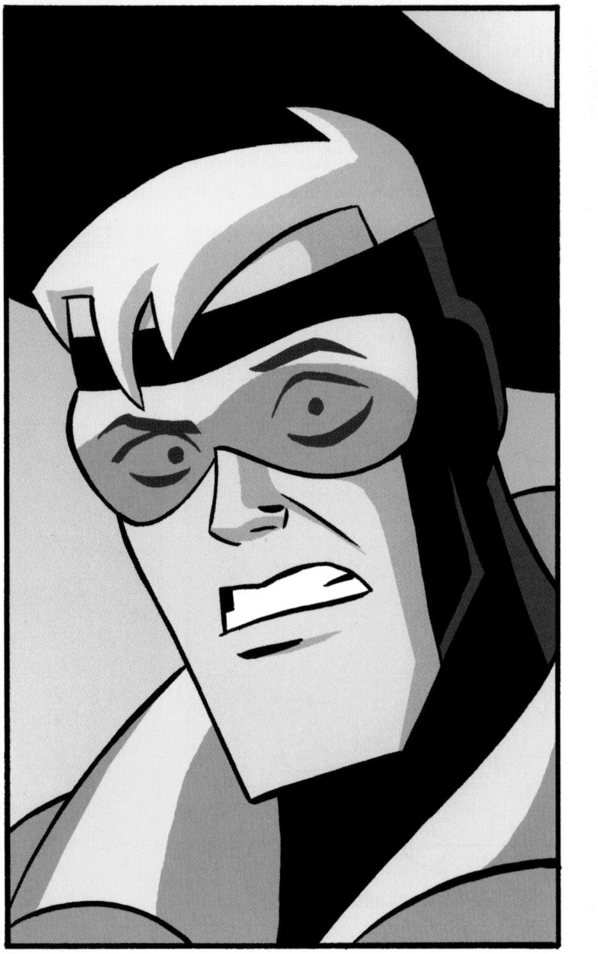

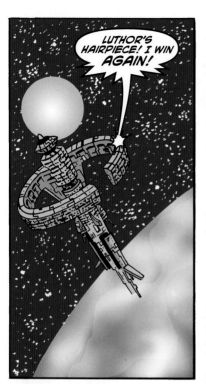

LUTHOR'S HAIRPIECE! I WIN *AGAIN*!

BOOSTER, I WAS *BLUFFING!* I CAN'T *BELIEVE* YOU FOLDED A *FULL HOUSE!* WHAT WERE YOU *THINKING?*

HEY, *TEAMWORK...* THAT'S WHAT THE JUSTICE LEAGUE IS ALL ABOUT.

HUH?

NEVER MIND, SUPERMAN...

JUST *DEAL.*

END.

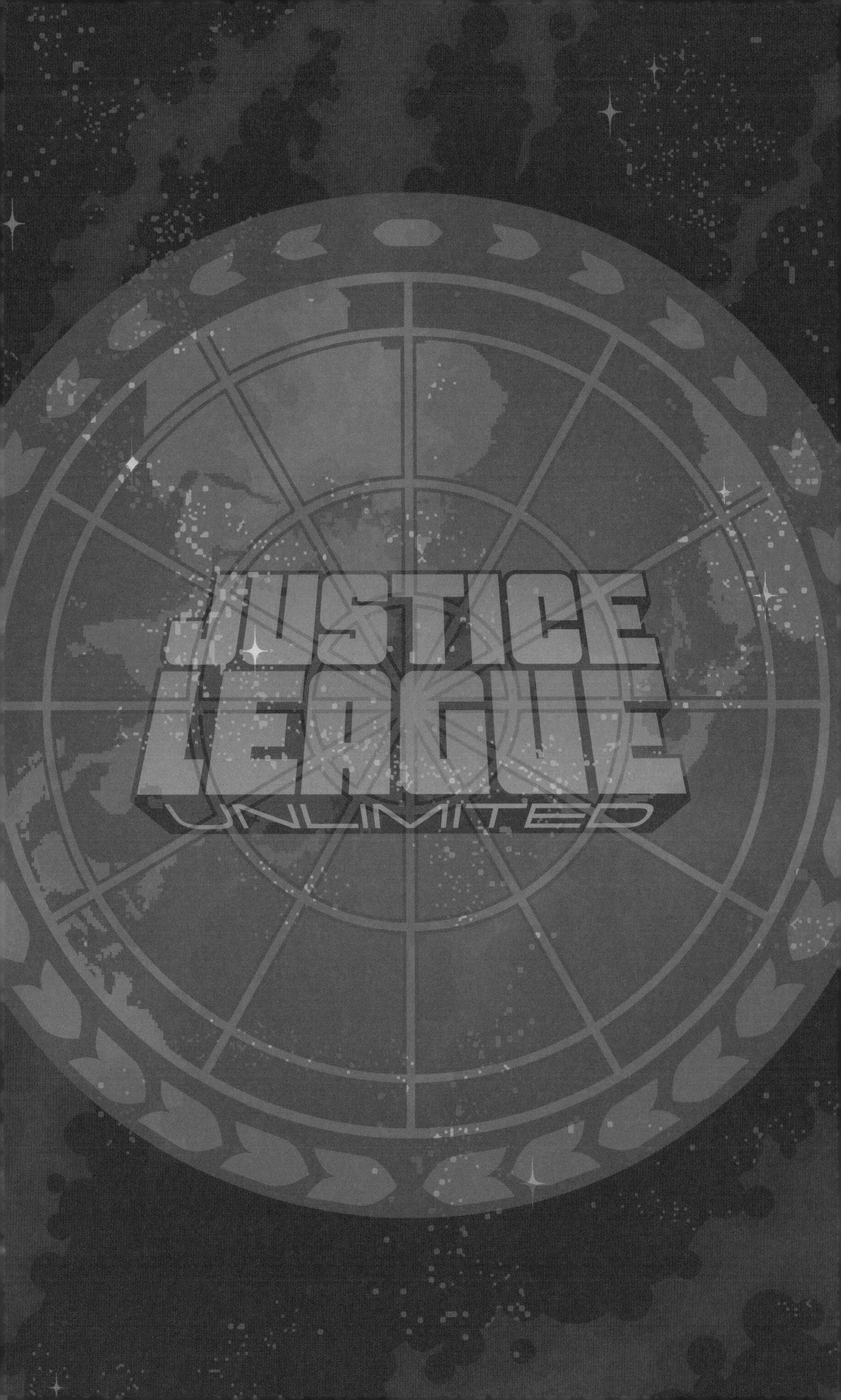
JUSTICE LEAGUE
UNLIMITED

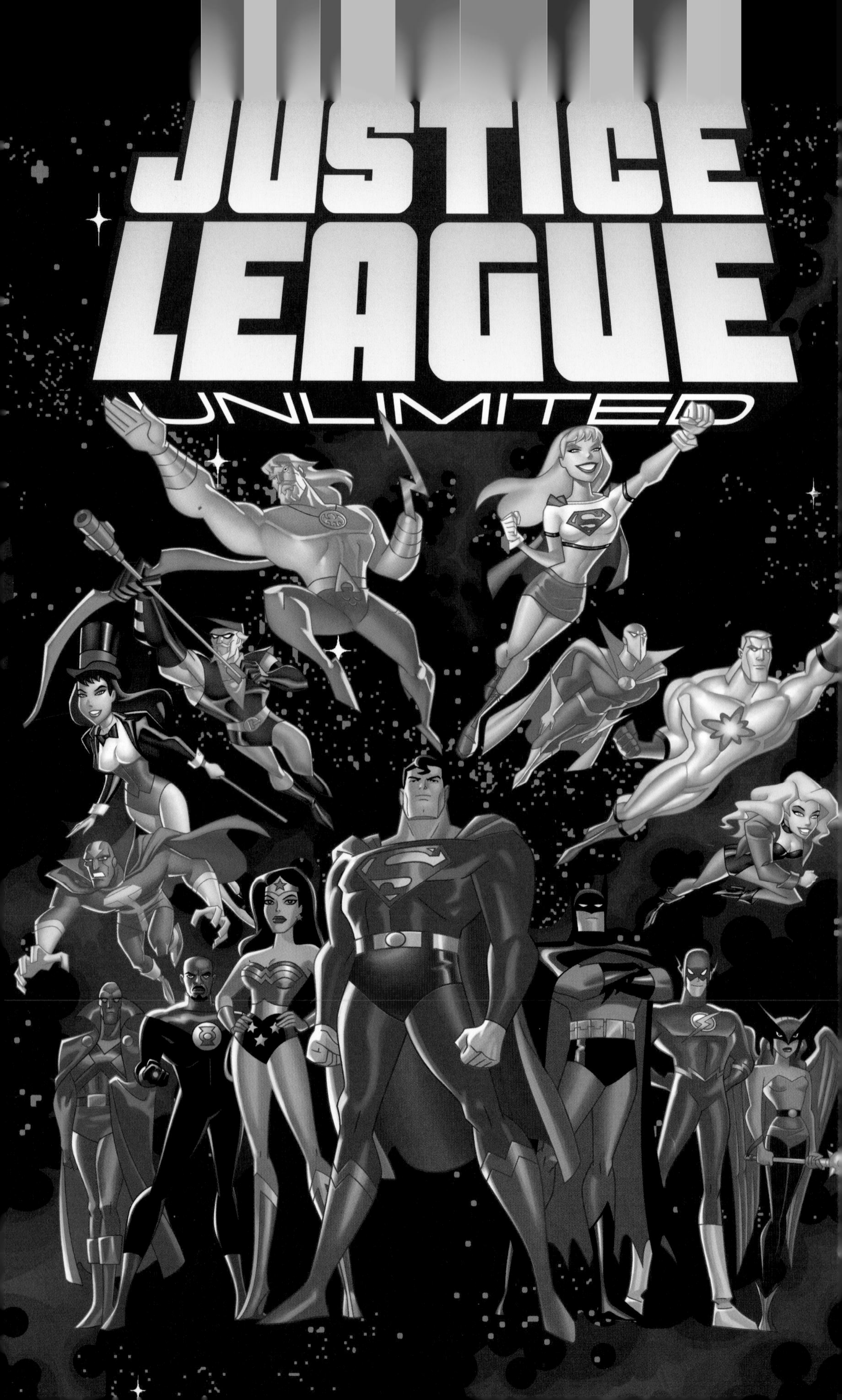
JUSTICE LEAGUE
UNLIMITED

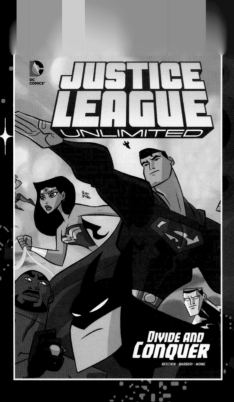

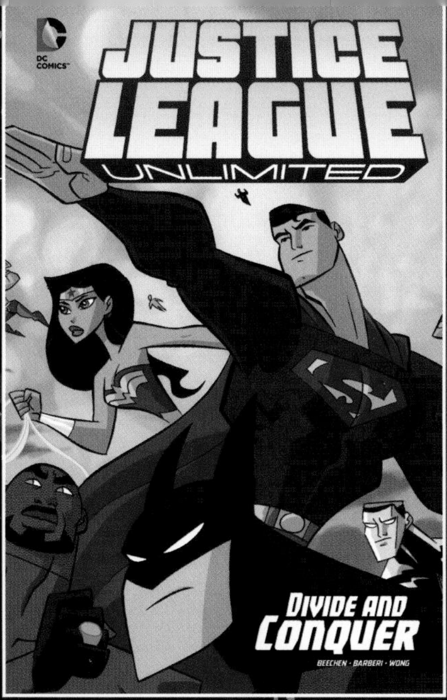
DC COMICS
JUSTICE LEAGUE
UNLIMITED
DIVIDE AND CONQUER
BEECHEN · BARBERI · WONG

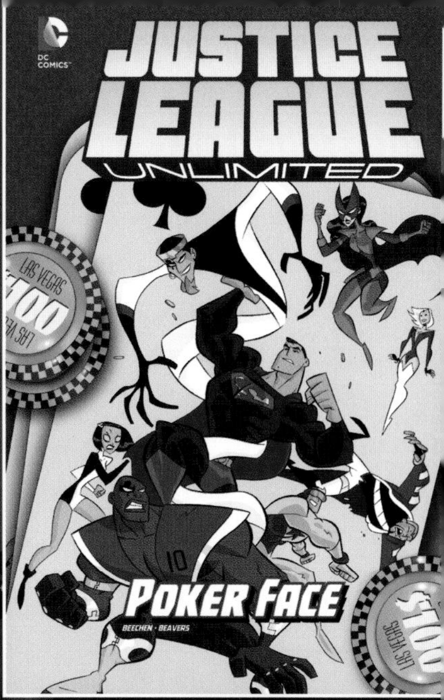
DC COMICS
JUSTICE LEAGUE
UNLIMITED
LAS VEGAS
100
POKER FACE
BEECHEN · BEAVERS

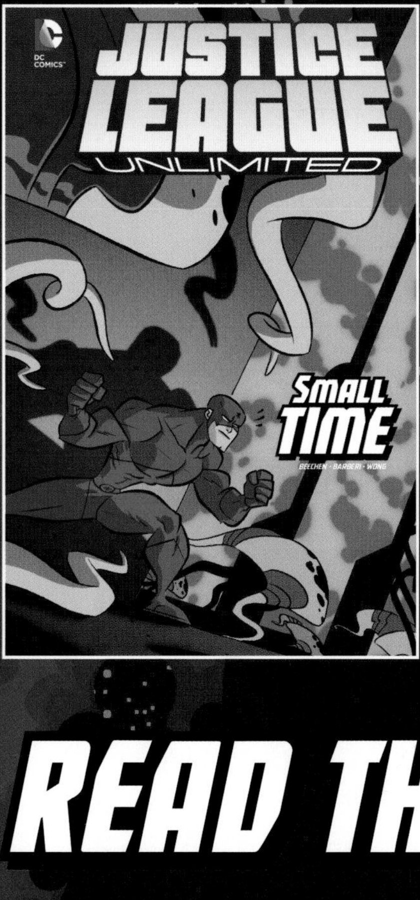
DC COMICS
JUSTICE LEAGUE
UNLIMITED
SMALL TIME
BEECHEN · BARBERI · WONG

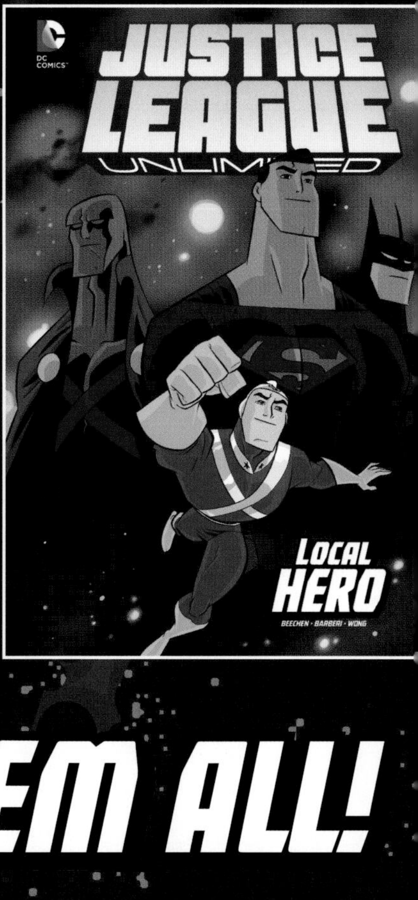
DC COMICS
JUSTICE LEAGUE
UNLIMITED
LOCAL HERO
BEECHEN · BARBERI · WONG

CREATORS

ADAM BEECHEN WRITER

Adam Beechen has written a variety of TV cartoons, including *Ben Ten: Alien Force*, *Teen Titans*, *Batman: The Brave and the Bold*, *The Batman* [for which he received an Emmy nomination], *Rugrats*, *The Wild Thornberrys*, *X-Men: Evolution*, and *Static Shock*, as well as the live-action series *Ned's Declassified School Survival Guide* and *The Famous Jett Jackson*. He is also the author of *Hench*, a graphic novel, and has scripted many comic books, including *Batgirl*, *Teen Titans*, *Robin*, and *Justice League Unlimited*. In addition Adam has written dozens of children's books, as well as an original young adult novel, *What I Did On My Hypergalactic Interstellar Summer Vacation*.

ETHEN BEAVERS ARTIST

Ethan Beaver is a professional comic book artist from Modesto, California. His best-known works for DC Comics include *Justice League Unlimited* and *Legion of Superheroes in the 31st Century*. He has also illustrated for other top publishers, including Marvel, Dark Horse, and Abrams.

WORD GLOSSARY

bluffing (BLUHF-ing)--pretending to know more about something than you really do

coincidence (koh-IN-si-duhnss)--a chance happening or meeting

crisis (KRYE-siss)--a time of danger or difficulty

distraction (diss-TRAKT-shuhn)--something that weakens one's concentration

flush (FLUHSH)--a poker hand where all five cards are the same suit but not in sequence

liege (LEEJ)--a fuedal lord

manipulate (muh-NIP-yuh-late)--to manage especially with intent to deceive

obnoxious (uhb-NOK-shuhss)--very disagreeable or offensive

pedestrian (puh-DESS-tree-uhn)--a person who is walking

poker (POH-kur)--a card game in which a player bets on the value of his or her hand

J.L.U. GLOSSARY

ENERGY BLASTS

As a super hero from the future, Booster Gold possesses advanced technology, including a power suit that is equipped with a force field and energy blasters.

SUPER-BREATH

Earth's yellow sun gives the Man of Steel many superpowers, including super-breath. Superman is able to condense and pressurize air in his lungs, then blast enemies with icy breath.

SUPER-SPEED

Also Known as the Fastest Man on Earth, the Flash is gifted with the power of super-speed, capable of outrunning danger, created tornadoes with his whirling arms, or vibrating through solid objects.

VISUAL QUESTIONS & PROMPTS

1. In comic books, sound effects (also known as SFX) are used to show sounds, such as an explosion. Make a list of all the sound effects in this book, and then write a definition for each term. Soon, you'll have your own SFX dictionary!

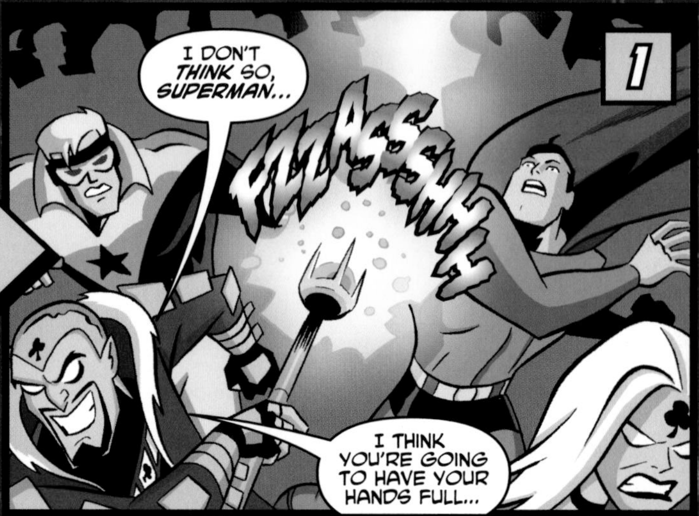
1
I DON'T THINK SO, SUPERMAN...
I THINK YOU'RE GOING TO HAVE YOUR HANDS FULL...

2. A person's physical gestures, poses, and expressions can sometimes indicate whether they are good or evil. Study the panel below. What clues led you to believe that these characters were evil?

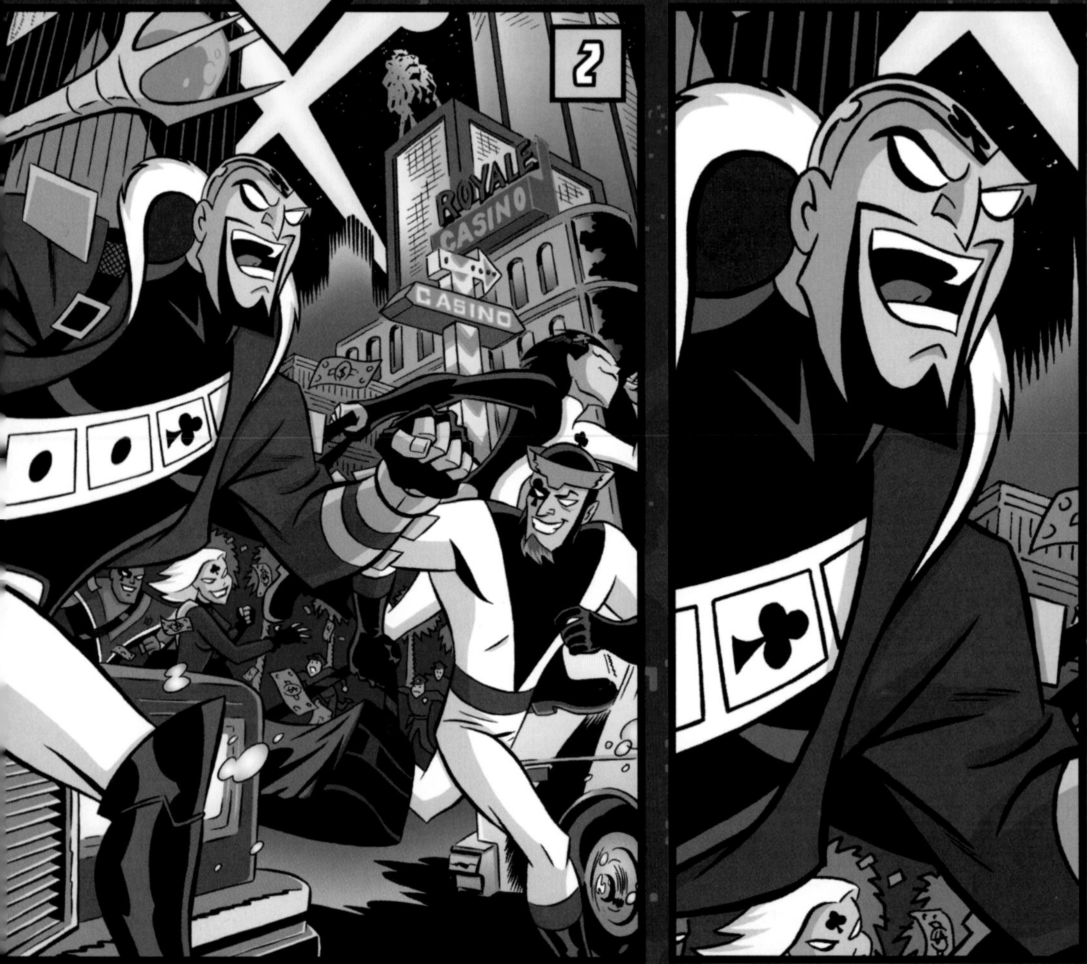
2
ROYALE
CASINO
CASINO

3. Who do you think is speaking in the first panel below? Explain how you were able to identify the speaker.

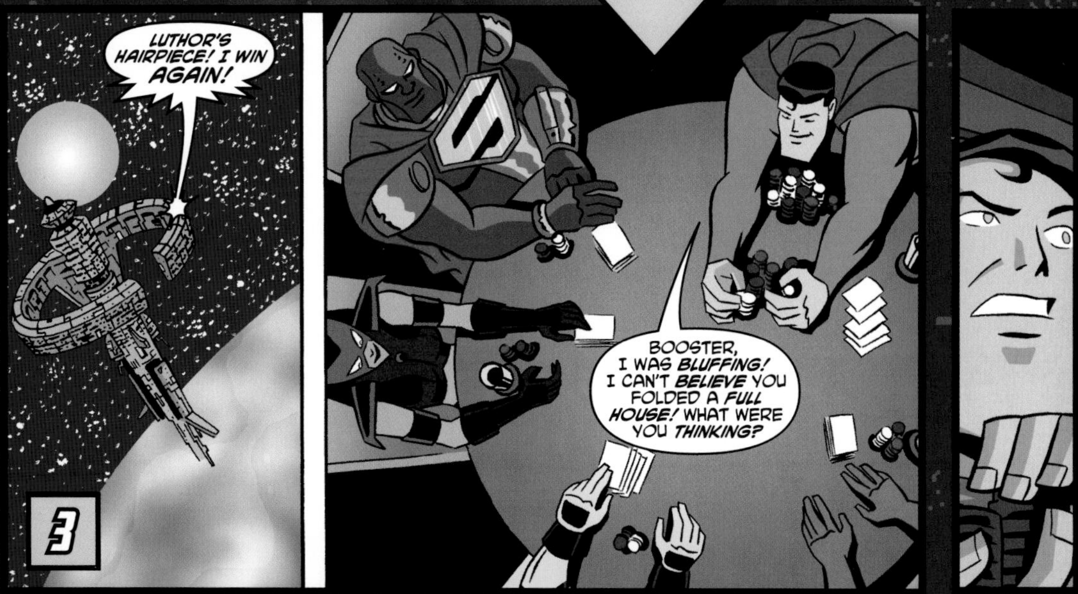
LUTHOR'S HAIRPIECE! I WIN AGAIN!
3
BOOSTER, I WAS BLUFFING! I CAN'T BELIEVE YOU FOLDED A FULL HOUSE! WHAT WERE YOU THINKING?

4. After reading this story, who do you think is the most powerful member of the Justice League? Do you think that character could have defeated Royal Flush Gang alone? Why or why not?

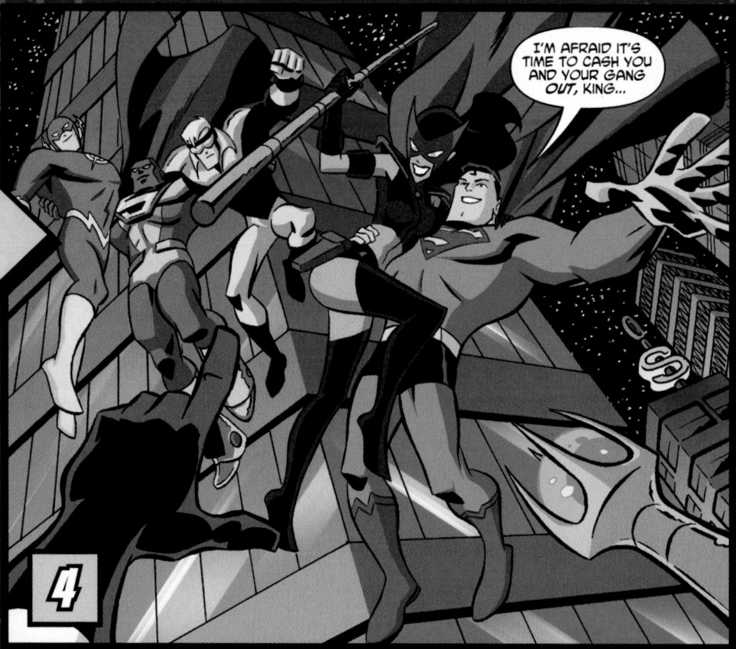
I'M AFRAID IT'S TIME TO CASH YOU AND YOUR GANG OUT, KING...
4

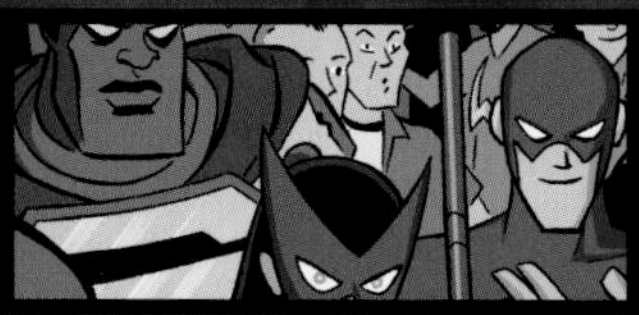

5. Why do you think Booster Gold is upset at the end of this story? Is he frustrated with Superman? Angry because he lost the poker hand? Explain your answer.

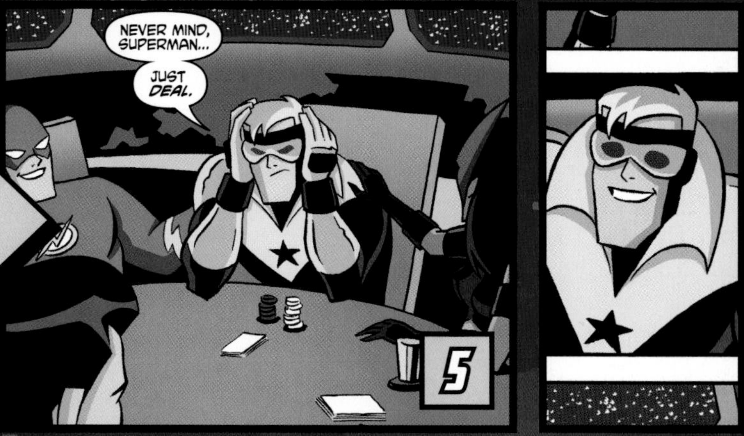
NEVER MIND, SUPERMAN...
JUST DEAL.
5

WANT EVEN MORE?

GO TO...

www.CAPSTONEKIDS.com

Then find cool websites and more books
like this one at www.facthound.com.

Just type in the BOOK ID:
9781434247148

Marshall County Public Library
@ Hardin
Hardin, KY 42048